ONE-WAY TO ANSONIA

ONE-WAY TO ANSONIA

A novel by
JUDIE ANGELL

BRADBURY PRESS   NEW YORK

Bradbury Press
An Affiliate of Macmillan, Inc.
866 Third Avenue, New York, N.Y. 10022
Collier Macmillan Canada, Inc.
Manufactured in the United States of America
1   3   5   7   9   10   8   6   4   2
The text of this book is set in 11 pt. Baskerville.

Library of Congress Cataloging in Publication Data:
Angell, Judie. One-way to Ansonia.
Summary: At the turn of the century, ten-year-old Rose
immigrates from Russia to America and eventually finds that
her emergence into adolescence brings employment,
marriage, motherhood, and self-determination.
1. Children's stories, American.   [1. Emigration and
immigration—Fiction.   2. Russian Americans—Fiction]
I. Title.
PZ7.A5824On   1985   [Fic]   85-5652
ISBN 0-02-705860-3

Contents

❦ ❦

For
AUNT ANNA ROGOFF COHEN
who remembers

At Grand Central Station
New York City

～～ ～～

December 1899

Rose Rogoff, holding her sleeping baby against one hip, set her suitcase on the floor and stepped up to the booth on whose window were lettered the words: Bureau of Information. She was glad she'd learned to read, no matter what they'd all said.

The booth was adjacent to the train shed and Rose turned for a moment to gape at the massive locomotives behind the gates to the tracks.

"May I help you?" the man in the booth asked. His moustache drooped and Rose thought his voice did, too. She drew in her breath.

"I have three dollars," she said in her best English. "Yes . . ."

"I want to go somewhere . . . where you can see mountains. And also trees. A small town. Where is that?"

The man arched his eyebrows. "You mean," he said, "you don't have a particular destination in mind?"

Destination, destination . . . Rose didn't know the word exactly, but she felt she caught its meaning.

"I don't know where it is I want to go. Only that it should be small, a nice town . . . with houses, not big buildings like here. Not crowded streets, with people yelling all the time. But—it doesn't have to be a rich town. I didn't mean *that*."

"So what you mean is," the man said, half-amused, half-annoyed, "anywhere you can go on three dollars. You and the baby."

Rose nodded.

"You're all alone?"

"That's right." Rose held her little boy tighter. The huge terminal represented everything Rose was anxious to escape: stone, metal, walls, crowds. The famous Vanderbilt landmark was undergoing renovations, but they wouldn't improve anything for her. Great arches, however beautiful, were still stone, still cold. And Rose wanted more daylight than could be seen through transom windows.

The man in the booth peered at her. "You want someplace here in New York? State, that is."

"Can I go to another state with three dollars?" Rose inquired eagerly. The possibility of *someplace else* intrigued her.

"Well . . . sure. You could go to New Jersey or Connecticut or—"

"Connecticut!" Rose cried. "Oh, yes!" Mr. Pratt, her night-school teacher, and his sister often talked about Connecticut. They went to parties there—lawn parties, beach parties . . . Rose knew nothing about Connecticut except that it sounded pretty. Lawns and beaches. And it wasn't New York! Since she'd arrived in America, Rose had never been out of the Lower East Side of the city; "New York" would always mean *ghetto* to her.

". . . somewhere in Connecticut," the man was mumbling. "Well, that narrows it down . . ."

The sarcasm was lost on Rose. "As far as the three dollars will go," she repeated.

"You have more? I mean, after you buy your ticket."

"More money? No, but I am not worried. I'll get it."

The man frowned at Rose over the window counter. "How old are you, anyway?" he asked. "Fifteen?"

"Seventeen," Rose answered stiffly, and then in a whisper, "almost."

"The baby yours?"

"Yes."

"And you're going on this trip all alone—with a baby—to somewhere you don't know, with no money, right?"

"That's right. But I said I'm not worried."

"Running away from your husband or something? You *got* a husband?"

"I'm not running away. I'm running *to*."

The man made a clicking noise with his tongue and frowned into Rose's face. Then he consulted some maps and schedules he had spread out in front of him. When he looked up again, two people had joined the line behind Rose. He became more businesslike.

"All right, Miss," he said. "Connecticut. Three dollars will take you as far as Ansonia."

"Aunt Sonya?"

3

"Right. Ansonia, Connecticut." He noticed her bewilderment. "It's the name of a town," he said slowly. "Like you said you wanted."

"Oh. I thought you meant someone's aunt."

The man smiled. "It's a small town. Couple factories, some stores, residential . . ."

"Mountains?"

"Well . . . hills, anyway. But pretty big hills. And trees, parks, yards . . . Nice little village green. All those New England towns have little greens . . . Used to be a conductor. Traveled through those towns."

A man behind Rose shifted his feet in line and coughed. The man in the booth drew himself up. "Yes or no, young lady?"

"Yes," Rose breathed.

"Understand, now—three dollars buys you a one-way ticket to Ansonia. One-way. Right?"

"One-way," Rose repeated. "Right."

"Ticket booths are over there." He indicated with his hand. "They've built a false front where the track gates are with a big clock at the top, see, because it's hard to read the original clock behind it. Your train leaves at eleven-thirty. Track sixteen. Keep an eye on that new clock, now."

"Eleven-thirty, track sixteen," Rose repeated. "I'll watch the clock. I'll watch *both* clocks!"

"Good luck," the man called as Rose turned away. Then he cleared his throat and said, "Next?"

4

ONE

1893

Moshe's Children ⌒

The little room was stuffy. Airless. It smelled of too
many people in one place for too long a time. Like
the boat, except it wasn't moving. No . . . not like the
boat . . .

Rose shifted from one foot to the other. She pushed
the toe of her shoe through the torn threads of the
rug.

"Stand still, Rose," her oldest sister, Hinde, warned.

"And be quiet," Yette, the next-in-line, added. "Papa
said we have to stay quiet."

"I am quiet," Rose said. "I'm just tired."

Meyer, the middle child and only boy in the family,
was carrying Baby Celia, six. "We're all tired, Rosele.
It's been a long day. But it won't be much longer . . ."
Baby Celia whimpered in his arms and he patted her
brown curls with his free hand. "Not much longer. I
hope . . ."

Rose smiled up at her big brother. He seemed even
more grown up than Hinde and Yette, though he was

just fourteen. He was the only one since their mother
died who called her by a pet name: Rosele. Little Rose.

"Meyer, what's taking so long?" she sighed. "This
dress itches!"

"Don't complain," Yette said. "At least you got to
change clothes. And you have a new dress, too. So
don't complain."

Rose bowed her head. Yette was right. Since they'd
stumbled off the boat at Ellis Island in New York
Harbor, there had been no time for anything. Papa
had met them, hugged them, scolded them and talked
at them without stopping even long enough to hear
about the scary part with Baby Celia. Meyer had tried
to tell him about it.

"We almost didn't get through, Papa!" he'd cried.
"Celia's eye was all red! They turn you back if you
have conjunctivitis!"

"But you did get through," their father answered,
pushing them into the crowds.

"Yes, but only because of Rose," Meyer said.

"You got through, that's what matters. Hurry, hurry!"

"Rose distracted the examiner," Meyer continued,
raising his voice as he tried to keep up with his father.
"She talked so much and so fast—she showed the
examiner her suitcase and said how she'd accidentally
hit Celia in the eye with a corner of it—"

"Meyer, be careful with that box," Hinde cautioned
as they stumbled along.

"I'm careful—I've got it. Anyway, Papa, Rose chattered so much at that examiner about her carelessness
and hurting Celia and our family and everything all
at once—the examiner just pushed us out of the way

and called, 'Next!' Rose thought quickly, Papa. The man hardly looked at Celia. I could hear my own heart beating—but it was Rose who got us through—"

Their father had hardly listened. He'd rushed them to this big building, shoving them all through the doorway and depositing them and their bundles of belongings in this small room. They had not eaten, washed or changed clothes. Except for Celia and Rose.

"Papa said there'll be lots of food at the wedding," Yette said. Rose looked up sharply. It was as if Yette had read her mind. But everyone was thinking about food. All they'd had on the boat through the two weeks of crossing was what they'd been able to bring aboard with them. The last time they'd had full stomachs was on the train—a two-day trip to Danzig, the free port from which they'd sailed.

Celia whimpered again. "I want to go to sleep, Meyer," she mumbled.

"You are asleep," Meyer said, smiling. "Don't you want to wake up and see your pretty dress? Rose has a new dress, too."

The dresses weren't new. They were little girls' bridesmaids' dresses, and they had been through many other weddings. Their lace hems were torn and Celia's sleeves had some buttons missing, but they were clean and nearly white and the two younger girls could still wear them. Rose's was a little tight. She was ten now and had grown quite a bit in the last year.

"Where did Papa get these dresses?" Rose asked.

"Don't ask. It doesn't matter," Hinde said. "You're just lucky to have a new dress for your papa's wedding."

7

"Papa's had a lot of weddings," Rose shrugged. Meyer smiled. Since their mother died three years before, their papa had married two other women. This woman was new, someone he'd met here, in America. They were to be married in a few minutes. Their papa had explained that bringing his children from the old country was a surprise for his wife at their wedding. That's why the five of them had to stay quiet and out of sight.

"What's her name again?" Rose asked. "Papa's new lady. What's her name?"

Hinde frowned. "He told us . . . I can't remember."

"He told us so much," Yette said. "He talked the whole time . . . He said we were lucky he brought us to America. He said we were lucky we had such a good papa who saved to bring his children to America. And on the night of his wedding, too! He said we were lucky."

Rose giggled. "He always says we're lucky. He said I was lucky when he got me that job in Reb Enahva's house, cooking for his family and cleaning up after his children. Papa said I was lucky then."

"Well," Yette sniffed, "you were. You were lucky to get a job. Leah Mersky wanted that job, too, but she didn't get it."

"Leah Mersky was six," Rose told her. "I was eight, I could do more. Don't be silly, Yette. It was Reb Enahva who was lucky. I was the best housekeeper in Neschviz."

Hinde frowned and Yette pursed her lips. "You're too fresh sometimes, Rose," Yette said.

"Mume!" Meyer cried suddenly, and Celia stirred and blinked her eyes.

"What?" Rose looked up.

"Mume!" Meyer repeated, and laughed. "That's her name! I remember now!" He looked at his bewildered sisters. "Papa's new wife!" he said, smiling and shaking his head. "Her name is Mume! Our new mother!"

The door opened and an elderly woman bustled in, her head covered with a knitted shawl.

"Is Celia here?" she asked. "Moshe told me Celia was here . . ."

"She's here," Meyer said, nodding at Celia in his arms. "Papa wants Celia?"

"He wants her," the woman said.

Celia wrinkled her nose. "No," she whined, snuggling against her brother's chest. "I don't want to go."

"Your papa wants you," the woman repeated. "You must come now. Come." She beckoned with her arm.

"Mey-er," Celia wailed.

"It's been a trying day for her," her brother explained to the woman. "We just docked this morning. We haven't eaten and we're tired. Celia's our baby . . . Her eye was red this morning . . . Maybe one of us could go to Papa instead of Celia . . ."

The woman frowned. "I only know Moshe sent me in here for Celia. Fanny wants to meet her."

There was silence. Meyer, Hinde, Yette and Rose all looked at each other.

"Who's Fanny?" Rose asked.

"Mume's daughter, of course," the woman answered. "Who else?"

"Go, Celia," Meyer said, putting her down. "Go to Papa. We'll see you inside."

"You come, too," Celia whimpered.

"No, just you, Celiale. Papa's wife's daughter wants to meet you."

Celia went, holding the woman's hand. A few minutes later, the door opened again and their papa—Moshe Olshansky—stood on the threshhold. His red hair and beard gleamed from brushing and from tonic. His eyes sparkled.

"It's time," he announced, beaming. "I'm to be married. My children are here with me in America. I must be the happiest man in the world."

"Papa?" Hinde said tentatively.

Moshe came toward her, smiling. Even the hitch in his walk was hardly noticeable. He touched Hinde's cheek.

"Yes, Hindele, my oldest child, my obedient girl, it's wonderful you can share my happiest moment with me, except for when I married your mother, may she rest in peace."

Hinde waited for him to finish. He usually addressed them in long sentences with many phrases. Rose noticed her papa hadn't mentioned his other two wives.

"Papa, when are we to meet Mume?" she asked.

"Before the wedding or after the wedding?" Yette asked quickly.

"After! After the wedding! I told you, you're a surprise! Surprises after, not before!"

"But what about Celia?" Rose wanted to know.

"Celia was no surprise."

"You mean you told Mume only about bringing Celia across the ocean? Not the rest of us?" Meyer asked. "I'm confused, Papa."

"After the wedding no more confusion," his papa answered. "After the wedding, food, singing, dancing . . ."

"Papa . . . we're so tired," Rose said. She yawned. She couldn't help it. "The boat . . . It was so hard on the boat . . . Now we're here . . . When can we go to sleep?"

"After you celebrate your papa's marriage to a wonderful woman in America then you can go to sleep. My daughter, Rose, who someday might be pretty if she stops biting her nails, you have a long time after you're dead to sleep . . ."

"Moshe!" someone called.

He turned. "Coming! I'm coming!" he called back. "Now, children, come and see me get married!" He beamed at them and disappeared into the next room.

The Wedding ⤳

"She's very small," Rose whispered to Yette next to her. "I bet I'm as tall as she is."

"Sh," Yette said. "It's just the way she's standing. Her shoulders are bunched up."

"If I were getting married my shoulders wouldn't be bunched up," Rose said.

Hinde said, "Sh!" to both of them and Yette blushed.

Suddenly, there was the muffled sound of the glass breaking inside the cloth as Moshe's foot came down hard on it, and the crowd of wedding guests cheered loudly. The groom breaking the glass—the symbol of a long married life.

"Hooray!" Meyer cheered with the others.

"He's broken three other glasses," Rose said, "and none of his married lives has been long."

"Maybe it will be different here in America," Meyer said.

"Maybe in America they will make him get a divorce before he marries someone else!" Hinde said, but Meyer gripped her shoulder. Their papa, Moshe, had suddenly appeared in front of them with his arm about the waist of his new wife, Mume.

"My sweet angel," Moshe said grandly to her, "here they are! Here are my other children whom all afternoon until the wedding I have been keeping in the next room as a surprise for you! They made no sound, quiet as small mice, so you shouldn't see them until now! Here is my Hinde, my Yette, my Meyer, my Rose. My Celia you know, she dances there with your Fannele. Tired she is, but see, she dances—"

Rose was staring at Mume's face. It was ghostly white under her bride's headdress. Mume's mouth was open. She was frowning at each of the four older children.

"Moshe," she said. Her voice was hoarse.

"My angel, yes!"

"You are telling me these are your children?"

"That's what I am telling you. I bring them as a surprise from Neschviz for the wedding. Two weeks they are traveling just for this!"

But Mume was waving her hand and shaking her

head. "Celia, you said! *One daughter*, my Fanny's age. You said Celia. *One daughter*, you said!"

Yette gasped aloud. Quickly she put her hand to her mouth.

"You never told her, Papa," Rose blurted. "You never told her you had other children at all!"

There was a silence in the hall. The dancing had stopped. The wedding guests were still.

"A surprise," Moshe said again. "I meant them as a surprise . . ."

"A surprise they are," Mume agreed. "Now where will your surprises sleep?"

"Mume!" Moshe cried. "Here is my Hinde, my Yette, my—"

"I heard," Mume said. "Celia I am ready for. My Fannele will have a sister her own age. The apartment on Hester, it's big enough for four. Four can manage. Four will manage. Eight will not. Moshe's children, how do you do. You'll have to live somewhere else." She folded her arms and glared at them.

Moshe looked around the hall. The wedding guests looked back at him. He opened his arms to all. "My children!" he cried, his eyes filling with tears. "Most of you are Neschvizer . . . You are all landsmen, countrymen . . . Where will my children live?"

No one answered. A fiddle began to play, then another.

Hinde, Yette, Meyer and Rose stood in the middle of the floor.

"By the end of the wedding you will have homes," Moshe said to them. "Do not worry."

Mume, tight-lipped and stiff-necked, turned away.

Moshe put his hand on the small of her back and eased her into the crowd. People had begun to dance again and talk among themselves.

" 'Do not worry,' " Yette repeated. " 'By the end of the wedding you will have homes.' " She shook her head as her eyes filled. "We don't have any place to sleep," she sobbed softly.

"We haven't slept in real beds for weeks," Hinde mumbled. "And we haven't washed. No wonder the new wife doesn't want us!"

"That's not why!" Rose turned to her sister. "It's not because we smell bad. It's because she didn't know about us! Papa never told her he had any other children! Only Celia, because she's six like Mume's daughter."

Yette wiped her eyes. "I'm so tired," she sighed.

"We're all tired," Meyer said. "Except Celia—look at her! She's dancing . . . She looks happy, doesn't she?"

Rose poked an elbow into Hinde's ribs. "Papa's waving at you," she said.

"At me?"

"He's calling 'Hinde!' Over there." Rose pointed and Hinde began to move, but Moshe reached them first, crossing the room in huge strides. Behind him trailed a small man in a baggy blue suit. Moshe pulled the man by his sleeve.

"Hinde, meet my good friend, Eli Skloots. You know the alleyway between Reb Yankel's house and Uncle Abraham's store back home?"

Hinde nodded.

"Well, after that alleyway there was a road that if you followed would take you up into the hills where the milk cows grazed?"

Hinde nodded. "Yes, Papa . . ."

"Well, on that road, halfway between the hills and the alleyway, the Skloots family lived!"

Hinde sighed. "Oh," she said.

"So they're landsmen, you see? Everyone here is landsmen. I can tell you where all their families lived at home."

Hinde blinked her eyes.

"Skloots will take you to his house," Moshe said suddenly. "You'll live with him. His wife is Zena, she's a midwife, and there are two nice girls, a little bit younger than you. They work in the Griffin Cap Factory. You'll work there, too."

Hinde looked at her brother and sisters. Their heads were bowed.

"Well?" her father said. "Tell Mr. Eli Skloots!" He urged her with his eyes. She knew what he meant.

"Thank you, Mr. Eli Skloots," she said, "for taking me into your home."

Eli Skloots looked at her with sad eyes. "A cousin of my wife's, Ethel Streller, she was living with us. But last week she got married, she moved out. You'll share the room with my girls, Anna and Lillian."

"Anna and Lillian," Hinde repeated.

"And *smile*, Hinde," Moshe said through his teeth, "like you always do. She's always smiling," he told Eli.

"Hinde? Always *smiling*?" Rose burst out. She would

15

have smiled herself, but Moshe glared at her and she tightened her lips.

Eli didn't seem to notice the exchange. "When we go home," he said to Hinde, "you come with us. You have your things? Not much things . . . ?"

"Not much . . ."

Eli nodded. "I'll find my wife," he said, "and tell her."

"I'll find someone for you, Yette," Moshe said. "And someone for you, Meyer. And you, Rose. Don't worry. How lucky you are, Hinde!" And he left them.

" 'How lucky you are, Hinde!' " Rose mimicked. "Always smiling, too!" Hinde glared at her the way Moshe had. Rose sighed. "Ah, Papa. America hasn't changed him much, has it?" But there was affection in her voice.

Moshe returned to them twice more. A family named Resnik would take Yette. They had a grocery store, but Yette would not work there. She, like Hinde, would work in a clothing factory doing piecework and paying some of her salary to the Resniks, the rest to Moshe.

Another family, the Lowensteins, would take Rose. But no factory work for Rose. The Lowensteins had two small children. Babies. Rose would take care of the children and help Mrs. Lowenstein in the house.

Rose sighed. "The best housekeeper in Neschviz," she muttered to herself.

"Rose . . ." her papa began, but Rose interrupted. "I know," she said quickly. "I'm lucky, Papa. Right?"

"*And?*" Moshe said, frowning.

"And . . . thank you, Papa."

Moshe nodded.

"How about me, Papa?" Meyer asked.

Moshe sighed and put a hand on his son's shoulder. "Lister will take you to drive his wagon, Meyer. You can sell for him the knives and the scissors and you can sharpen the ones the people bring you. But Lister, he has no room in his place for you, Meyer. His wife, his daughter, his brother's daughter, his son and his son's wife and their baby, they all live with him. You'll have to sleep in the wagon . . ." He shook his head. It was the best he could do. "The wagon, it has a cover made of oilcloth and canvas. And it's parked in the stable with the horse. With feather blankets at night . . . You'll be warm . . ."

"It's all right, Papa," Meyer said softly.

"You can go inside to eat . . ."

"It's all right," Meyer repeated.

"Meyer's not so lucky," Rose whispered, but her father heard her and frowned. Rose blushed.

"Meyer!" Celia raced up to them, holding another little girl by the hand. "Look, this is Fanny. She's my new sister. Mume says we're going to go to school together!"

Rose drew in her breath. Celia would go to school!

"That's wonderful, Celiale," Meyer said, and bent to kiss her.

"Fanny's already been to school! She was born here!"

Hinde and Yette looked at each other, then at Fanny. Six years old and born here, in America. They were both thinking of children they would have who would be born here. Would they go to school, too? None of the Olshansky children had ever gone to school . . .

Sunrise ～

Rose was jerked awake.

She had fallen asleep in a corner of the hall. The music had stopped. Yette, Hinde and Meyer were nowhere to be seen. Even her father was gone. Across the room, she caught a glimpse of the old woman she'd seen earlier, hurrying Celia and Fanny out the door.

Rose looked up into the face of a strange man.

"It's time to go," the man said. "The wedding is over. It's sunrise."

Rose blinked.

"Get up," the man said. "My wife is waiting. She needs help with the babies."

Rose got up without a word. Mr. Lowenstein had come to take her to his home.

"You aren't very big," he said, looking her over. "Clothes for a whole family are heavy when they're wet . . ."

Rose refrained from rubbing her sleepy eyes. "I can do it," she said. "I've done it since I was eight."

"Since you were eight, eh?" Mr. Lowenstein frowned. "You don't look much older than that now. Are you sure you're twelve?"

Rose's eyes widened. Her father had told Mr. Lowenstein she was twelve! Oh, Papa—twelve!

"Well?" Mr. Lowenstein said.

Rose chewed her lip. "I can do the work," she said, and added, "sir."

Mr. Lowenstein smiled. Rose noticed his teeth were black.

"Good," he said. "We'll go home. You'll take care of Louis and Minna. You'll help my wife. You'll see to my house."

He took her elbow. Quickly she looked around the emptying hall for a last glimpse of a familiar face. But there was no one.

1895

"Spotless" ⌒

Rose ran all the way to her father's Hester Street apartment, took the stairs two at a time, and pulled the door open without knocking. Breathing heavily, she dropped her suitcase and confronted Moshe and Mume's shocked faces.

"I'm not going back," she said.

"Back?" Mume bleated. "Back? To Lowensteins'?"

Rose nodded.

"In you burst? No knock?" Moshe waved his arm. "Stop this foolishness, Rose. Now. Pick up your suitcase. Go to Lowenstein and apologize."

But Rose tightened her mouth and stood still.

Mume's face was purple. "What do you mean, you won't go back to Lowensteins'!" she bellowed. "Imagine! An eleven-and-a-half-year-old girl telling her own papa what she will and will not do!"

"And *why* won't you go back to Lowenstein, who was kind enough to give you a roof over your head for more than a year?" Moshe asked, studying his daughter.

"Ever since your papa and I have been married," Mume broke in, "the Lowensteins took care of you. Brought you to their home the night you came to America. Gave you food and a bed. *And* they have a big place! Four rooms! Not like us with barely enough room for us and Fanny and your father's daughter Celia! No one we know has such a place as the Lowensteins!"

"Let the girl answer, Mume," Moshe said, still leaning back in the wooden chair.

Rose kept her head down. She wouldn't look at Mume, wouldn't look at her father. Rose kept her eyes on the floor, kept her lips tight-shut and shook her head slowly.

Moshe took a sip of tea. He looked at his daughter over the rim of the glass. He wished he were drinking something stronger, but there was no schnapps in the flat. Moshe was tired. He wanted to sleep. His daughter coming here this late at night was an unexpected problem and he had enough problems, not the least of which was Mume. Her shrill voice, badgering the girl, was piercing his brain.

"To leave people like the Lowensteins!" Mume wailed. "In the middle of the night yet!"

"Sharrup!" Moshe boomed, using his new American silencing word. There was silence.

"So here you are, Rose," he said finally.

"Here I am, Papa."

He nodded. "So. The Lowensteins?"

"Don't make me go back there, Papa."

"You were lucky, Rose. Four rooms, like Mume told you. What could be so bad? Rose?"

"I kept those four rooms spotless," Rose said evenly. "I had Louis and Minna with me all the time. I washed, mended, pressed all their clothes. They were the cleanest children on Ludlow Street. I bought the food. I cooked it, I cleaned up. Every other day I scrubbed the floor till you could eat from it."

"So? What was Ida Lowenstein doing all this time?" Mume interrupted. "Lying in bed, combing her hair?"

"She was there," Rose answered softly. "She was there, yelling at me, telling me how to clean, wash, mend, cook . . . Telling me what a bad job I was doing."

"Rose, you didn't do a bad job . . . ?" Moshe asked.

"I told you, Papa. What do you think?"

"I think you did a good job. The best housekeeper in Neschviz. So. This is why you're home, Rose? Because you did this work that every woman and girl does? Because the wife of Lowenstein, she yells? After a year and more, this is why you come to me?"

"No, Papa. That's not why."

"Why, then?" Mume demanded.

"Sometimes," Rose said, and her voice faltered. "Sometimes . . . Mrs. Lowenstein went out. To visit. Her sister . . ." Rose looked at the floor.

"This is a reason to leave?" Mume shrilled.

"Sharrup," Moshe said. "So, why then, Rose?"

But Rose could not look at them.

"You tell me a good reason," Moshe said, "and I won't take you back to Lowenstein's place right now. So tell me."

Rose kept her head down, but her body stiffened, as if she were saying, If you take me back there, you'll have to carry me the entire way.

Moshe looked at his wife, then back at his daughter. "Listen, Rose," he said, "tonight you can sleep here."

Mume exhaled loudly through her nose.

Moshe went on. "Tonight, you sleep here, in the room with the girls. Go wake one of them and share the bed."

"Celia!" Mume cried. "Wake your *father's* daughter!"

Rose nodded. She picked up her suitcase—the same old cloth one she'd brought on the boat from Neschviz, still with the same things inside, except for one shawl she'd managed to crochet for herself during the year and a half she'd spent at the Lowensteins'. It was a lovely thing and resembled a large web of cream-colored snowflakes.

Mume pointed her finger stiffly. "It's that door," she said. "And don't you wake up Fanny. You be quiet."

Rose did not remind her that her own voice had probably roused everyone in the building, but instead slipped quietly into the girls' bedroom and closed the door.

"She's not a good girl, Moshe," Mume said, not even trying to whisper. "She doesn't answer when you talk to her. What kind of daughter is that? I still don't know why she left that good place you found. Ida Lowenstein is a snob, but still! Four rooms . . ."

"I don't think it was Ida," Moshe said thoughtfully, staring straight ahead.

"What do you mean?" Mume asked, leaning toward him.

"Rose *is* a good girl. She would say if she could. She didn't say. It was something she couldn't speak about."

Mume frowned. "So what couldn't she speak about? What? Why didn't you take her back there like you said you would? She didn't give you a reason . . . You asked her for a reason . . ."

"You talk too much," Moshe said absently. "I have heard you talk enough today. Go to bed, Mume."

"But—"

"Go to bed, Mume, I told you!"

For a long time after Mume had left the kitchen, Moshe sat at the table. His eyes seemed to be focused on the gleaming brass candlesticks that were Mume's prized possessions, but he wasn't seeing them at all . . .

Rose and Celia ⌇

The little girls' bedroom was dark and Rose couldn't tell which bed was Celia's. As she stood, trying to decide which child's sleeping form was her sister's, Celia suddenly sat up.

"Over here, Rose," she whispered excitedly, and as Rose went to her, Celia threw her arms around the older girl's neck. "I'm so glad you're here!" she cried.

"Shh, Celiale . . . You'll wake Fanny . . ."

"Fanny can sleep through her Mama's yelling. I never can. Why did you leave Lowensteins'?"

"I don't want to talk about it, Celia."

"All right. I'm just glad you're here."

"I won't be able to stay, Celia . . ."

"Yes, you will! Where else would you go?"

Rose stood up and began to get undressed. "I guess I'll leave that to Papa. Now you'd better try to go to sleep. You have school in the morning, don't you?"

"Yes . . . But maybe I'll stay home tomorrow. To be with you."

"No, no. You mustn't do that. You're very lucky to be able to go to school, Celia. Never forget that."

"I know. I like it. Fanny doesn't, though . . ."

"Fanny will appreciate it later on." Rose slipped into the bed beside her sister. "Sleep now, Celiale," she breathed. "We'll see what the morning brings . . ."

At Lister's Wagon ⟿

A moment ago it had been dark. A thick, black dark that could almost be touched. Now, with only the smallest hint of dawn, shapes could be seen, colors and tones distinguished, and surroundings became familiar again.

Meyer Olshansky, fifteen and a half, lay in the back of a wooden wagon, staring at the beams of the stable above him. The air was heavy with the smell of horse, of hay and manure, of metal and of dank, rotting wood.

Meyer grunted as he stretched his cramped legs and hung his feet over the end of the wagon. He pulled his blankets tight around him against the early April chill and shivered.

It was his job to feed the horse, who slept so close

to him he could reach out and pat her nose if he stood up in the wagon.

As if to remind him of his obligation, Molly, the horse, snorted loudly.

"I hear you, Molly," Meyer said, "but give me a minute more. This early no one needs a knife."

In answer, the horse snorted again and stamped a front hoof.

"Oh, all right . . ." Meyer struggled to a sitting position. "What will you do without me," he asked the horse, "when I finally have a place indoors?" He began to climb out of the wagon. "Don't tell me . . . I know. Lister will have someone else to sleep in his wagon and sharpen his knives and axes and scissors and . . . feed . . . his . . . horse!" Meyer jumped to the ground. "Well," he continued as he filled a nearby bucket with stale grain, "someday I will have a place of my own. And enough money to take care of my sisters properly. Here, Molly . . ."

He held the bucket so that the horse could put her nose into it comfortably. "Do you believe me, Molly?" Meyer asked. The horse made crunching and slurping noises inside the bucket. "Well, I will. Whether you believe it or not. Hinde and Yette will probably be married by then . . ."

Molly snuffled, nearly knocking the bucket out of Meyer's hands.

"They'll have good husbands to take care of them," Meyer continued. "But Rosele and Celiale . . . Well, Rose won't have to work in anyone's house, ever again. Except her own. And Celia will have nice clothes, not

Fanny's leftovers that Mume makes her wear . . ." The horse lifted its head. "Are you through, Molly? Do you want some water?"

He dumped the uneaten grain from the bucket and pulled his sweater down from where he had tossed it over the side of the wagon. Carrying the empty bucket, he stretched again and went to the door, lifting the iron latch with his free hand.

The spring air smelled sweet and cool at this early hour and Meyer sniffed it eagerly as he walked toward the water pump in the street and began to crank it for Molly's morning drink.

At the Sklootses' ~~~

Several blocks away, fourteen-year-old Anna Skloots rolled over in bed, gently nudging her sister, Lillian. They both opened their eyes.

"Is it morning already?" Lillian mumbled.

Anna sighed. "I think so. I hear noises."

The only window in their room faced a brick wall and let in no light. There was no way to tell the time of day.

"Is Hinde awake?" Lillian asked.

"Yes." The answer came from the bed next to the sisters'. Hinde Olshansky would have it to herself until the Sklootses took in another female boarder. "I'm awake. I hear your mama in the kitchen . . ."

Zena Skloots had been up since dawn, beginning her baking for Shabbos, her washing of clothes in the water from the communal basin down the hall of the tenement. The night before, she had been out late, delivering twins for the Levins one street away.

". . . but I don't hear voices," Hinde finished. "Your papa is gone."

Eli Skloots had already taken his pushcart of dry goods to Canal Street.

"Ah, then it's morning," Lillian sighed.

There was a sharp rap on their door. "Up," Zena said, just once, and then her footsteps receded.

"It's morning," Anna repeated as all three girls sat up in bed. "And time to work."

Their jobs at the Griffin Cap Factory consisted of stitching all sorts of linings into all sorts of caps: yachting caps, golf caps, thick wool caps favored by old men and schoolboys. It was piecework and it was hard work, eyestraining work. When the girls came home, they helped make the knitted and crocheted things Eli sold from his cart.

"Rose has *the* job," Hinde said as she and Lillian and Anna buttoned the many buttons on their shirtwaists and pulled on their long skirts. They dressed quickly because of the chill in the morning air. "She gets to stay home and take care of babies. I'd like that, instead of clatter-clatter-clatter—"

"Push, lift, push," Lillian laughed, imitating their routine with their sewing machines. "I don't know, Hinde. I don't know if I'd like to be doing someone else's washing and cleaning and mopping up of babies' bottoms all day long . . ."

Anna smiled at her younger sister. "Well, you're not quite twelve yet, Lillian. There's time for all that."

"Rose is Lillian's age." Hinde reminded them. "And she's been doing housework for almost four years. She's very good at it and I think it's a much better occupation than putting linings in fancy caps!" Hinde smoothed down her skirt. "I'm nearly eighteen and I'd like to be thinking about mopping up a little baby's bottom . . . Wouldn't you, Anna?"

"Girls!" Zena called from the kitchen. "It's late! Your coffee's getting cold! Hurry!"

"Coming, Mama!" Anna called back. "I don't know about babies yet, Hinde . . . But I think about getting married . . ." Her face reddened and she couldn't help her widening smile.

"To *Meyer!*" Lillian giggled. "We know . . ."

"Oh, yes," Hinde said, making a face, "go keep house in my brother's wagon, Anna—"

"*Girls!*"

"We're coming!"

At the Resniks' ◢

As Hinde and Meyer were getting ready for work, their sister Yette had already begun hers. The Resniks, with whom she boarded, had a three-month-old collicky infant. Mrs. Resnik, never a healthy woman herself, took care of the baby and the other three children during the day while Yette was sewing at her shirtwaist factory. In the afternoons, the whole family helped in the Resniks' grocery store. But early in the morning, when the baby cried, it was Yette who tended to it so that Mrs. Resnik could get some extra rest. Mr. Resnik was at work in the store by that time.

As Yette sat and rocked the baby while the other Resnik children were washing their faces down the hall, she kept herself warm with a special thought. Sometime during the next two weeks, Yette Olshansky would become seventeen years old. One of those days would be her birthday.

Very few birth records had been kept in Neschviz. Family members approximated birthdays. They would point to each child and say, this one was born right after Yom Kippur, or, that one arrived when we harvested, or, this one came during the time of the great aunt's funeral. Yette knew that April was her birthday time. Back home in the *shtetl*—in Neschviz—the children would get a special sweet at their birthday time. If someone remembered.

"Maybe it's *today*," Yette whispered to the baby in her arms. "Sweet baby," she cooed, "maybe today is my birthday. None of us are together now, so probably no one will think of it—but in honor of the occasion, I am going to buy for myself a sugar bun at the bakery before I go to work. And I'll take you with me!"

Suddenly, the front door burst open and a small girl raced from the hall into the flat.

"Yette, Mikey took my shoe! He took my shoe! Make him give it back!" she cried.

"Becky," Yette began, but the little girl persisted, hopping on one shod foot.

"Make him give it to me! I have to go to school! Where's Mama? *Maaaaaa*-ma!"

The infant in Yette's arms woke up and began to

howl. The younger brother, Mikey, hurried into the flat and slapped at his sister Becky's curls, causing her to cry louder and Mikey to giggle uncontrollably.

Yette stood up. "Stop it!" she shouted. "Stop it, both of you! Look what you've done to your baby sister. And your mama so sickly and trying to rest! You should be ashamed of yourselves!"

The racket stopped. The two Resnik children hung their heads.

"That's better. Now where's Ruth?" Ruth was the third oldest in the Resnik family.

"Still washing . . ."

"You children are older. You should be helping her. Becky, go get her. Mikey, you go fix that collar of yours and have some bread before school. And give Becky her shoe! Now go!"

They went, but the baby continued to cry. Yette rocked and crooned to her.

Ah, Papa, she thought. How things have changed in just a year and a half. We all stay with other people's families, not our own. At least in Neschviz we all returned home at night, had supper together . . . We were a family . . . She thought of each of them on this spring morning: Hinde, Meyer, Rose, Celia . . .

The baby in her arms was still crying. Yette glanced nervously at the closed door behind her. In the small bedroom, her landsman, Mrs. Resnik, was trying to get the rest she needed to regain her strength. Yette kissed the baby's forehead and rocked harder.

"No time for a sugar bun today," she whispered. "But maybe today isn't my birthday. Maybe it's to-morrow . . ."

"God Takes Away, but He Also Gives"

Moshe made his way through the streets slowly. His bones hurt and his limp was more pronounced. The day was growing warm, but Moshe didn't notice. He was looking for Eli Skloots.

Moshe and Eli were friends. Landsmen. They played cards together, drank together, argued, prayed and laughed together. Eli Skloots had given Moshe's daughter Hinde a bed. He had no other boarder now, Moshe knew. Maybe Skloots would take Rose.

He found Eli at his pushcart on Canal Street. Eli was folding scarves and shawls, getting ready to start his day. They greeted each other.

"So. Skloots," Moshe said, limping up to the cart.

"So. Olshansky. How is it with you?" Skloots answered as he folded and piled, folded and piled. He held up a shawl, grinning. "Nice, yes? Your Hinde does nice work. My Lillian does nice work. But Anna?" He kissed his finger tips. "She has real talent!"

Moshe nodded. "It's good," he said, "but you should see what my Rose can do."

"Oh, yes?"

"God blessed her hands Himself. She crochets . . . Like an angel."

"So how is it with Rose?" Eli asked, and Moshe saw his chance.

"Not so good, Eli, not so good." He waved his fingers. "I won't take your time with it."

Eli Skloots stopped folding. "Take my time," he said. "What is it with Rose?"

Moshe raised his eyes to the heavens. "At Lowenstein's she cleans, she cooks, she minds the babies, she washes—"

"So? What woman doesn't do that?"

"But she doesn't get to use her magic hands, Eli! Her magic hands! The doilies she makes, the shawls, the spreads, the tablecloths—" He shrugged mightily. "Her God-given talent is wasted there!"

Eli stroked his chin. "She's good?" he asked.

"More than good."

"*More* than good," Eli repeated, nodding. Then he exhaled. "Hinde and Lillian and Anna, they work at Griffin Cap all day. At night they sew for me. They could use help . . ." He continued to nod. "Anna and Lillian, they share a bed. Hinde, she sleeps alone in the other one. Rose could share Hinde's bed . . ."

Moshe wiped a tear from one eye with the hem of his jacket. "And the sisters . . . my two daughters . . . they could be together," he said.

"Maybe Rose would leave Lowenstein and come to us," Eli said. "Would she leave those four big rooms, a bed of her own . . . ? Would she do that, Moshe?"

"For a chance to sew for you, Eli? For a chance to sew for you? She would leave a king's palace!"

"Well . . . you ask. You ask Lowenstein, I'm sure he'll have a *kanipshen*, a fit all over the floor . . ."

"I'll ask," Moshe said. "You'll probably have Rose by tomorrow." And blinking back tears, he limped off, leaving Eli to ready his wares. "So, God takes

33

away, but He also gives." Moshe ticked off his new blessings: "Rose will have a good place to live. She will be with Hinde. Mume will be happy and she won't nag. I didn't have to tell Skloots that Rose already left Lowenstein's . . . I didn't have to tell him why. God has taken from Rose, but He has given, too . . . Rose is lucky."

And Moshe started off to his carpentry job. His children provided him with weekly support so he could afford to take his time.

Celia and Fanny ⌒

"Papa left early this morning," Celia said as she and Fanny walked to school together, dragging their books over their shoulders in two straps made from strips of old shirts. Fanny carried a paper sack in her other hand.

"Yes, he's usually still sleeping when we leave," she giggled.

"But Rose didn't go with him. Rose is still at home," Celia said happily. "Her name is a flower and she came home as the season for flowers begins!"

Fanny made a face. "No flowers grow here, Celia. And to prove it, Rose won't be able to stay."

"Why not? Rose said that, too. Why can't she stay with us? We have room . . ."

Fanny bit her lip. She was sorry she'd spoken because Celia looked so upset. But still, it was true about Rose, and Celia might as well learn it from her new sister and best friend.

34

"Why can't she stay?" Celia repeated.

"Oh . . . you know how Mama is . . ."

Celia didn't answer. She knew.

"I'm sorry, Celia," Fanny said. "I like Rose. I wish she could stay. She does my braids a lot better than Mama does. Mama pulls so hard she stretches the skin on my face!"

Celia laughed.

"It must have been nice to grow up in a big family," Fanny said. "To have a brother and so many sisters . . . I'm glad I have you now, Celia. I'm glad my mama and your papa got married so we could be sisters."

Celia nodded. "Oh, it was nice!" she said, remembering. "Hinde and Yette were crabby sometimes, but they took good care of the family. And Rose made me pretty things to wear when I was a baby. And Meyer . . ." Celia smiled to herself. "Meyer always carried me when I got tired . . ." Celia's smile faded as she turned to Fanny. "Oh," she said quickly, "all that doesn't mean I don't love you, Fanny! You're a wonderful sister to me! And you're the only sister I ever had that was my age."

Fanny nodded and they walked in silence for a while. Suddenly, Celia cried, "Look!" and pointed ahead of them. "See that sign?"

"Which sign?"

"Way down there. Across the street. It says Cigars!"

Fanny squinted. She'd inherited her mother's nearsightedness. "So?" she asked.

"So, Fanny, I can read it! Cigars! C-I-G-A-R-S," she spelled in her broken English.

"Good," Fanny said, sounding a little like her mother as well. "Now you know where to buy cigars if you want them. I knew they sold cigars there before I went to school. I don't need to read, Celia. I don't know why we have to go to school, anyway. We'll just get married and keep house like Mama . . . And I would so much love to sleep late . . ."

"Oh, I like school," Celia said. "Rose says how much she wishes she could go. She said for me to learn for both of us."

Fanny stopped walking. She held out her paper sack to Celia. "There's cake in here," she said. "Mama gave it to me to eat in school. You take it."

"Oh, no, Fanny—"

"Please, Celia, please! I want you to take it. She never gives you anything until supper. *Please!*"

Celia smiled. "Let's break it in half," she suggested. "Then we'll each have some."

Fanny put her books down on the sidewalk. Then she reached into the sack so that Celia couldn't see and she broke the cake unevenly, taking the bigger half out for Celia. "But . . . don't tell Mama, though," she added.

At the Olshanskys' ⟶

Mume Olshansky squinted her eyes and peered out of her kitchen window at the alley below. One of the old men, standing near his pushcart below her, sold eyeglasses for thirty-five cents, but Mume had never considered buying a pair. She was tight with her pennies and vain, besides.

Mume was looking for her husband. Though she couldn't recognize him clearly, she knew she would be able to pick him out of the bustle of people in the alley and on the street by his bright red hair and beard, and by the way his body hitched to one side when he walked.

She pulled the skin under her eyes tight, to narrow them into slits. She was sure it improved her focus, but she never did it in front of her husband.

"Hurry up, hurry," Mume muttered through her teeth and craned her neck. Late-afternoon sun glinted off the rooftops. She couldn't see him.

Mume needed Moshe to be home. She couldn't handle the girl, Rose, by herself. The brat had come home the night before, telling them—Moshe and Mume—that she wouldn't go back to the Lowensteins', telling them she was finished there. Mume made a noise with her lips. Finished! Imagine! That fresh young girl leaving a beautiful four-room place like the Lowensteins' and refusing to say why! And where was that man!

Mume was waiting for news that Moshe had found another home for Rose. She'll never find a place as good as she had, Mume thought sourly. Serves her right.

During the morning, Rose had helped Mume get the little girls ready for school and then helped with the housework. But though Mume had asked what seemed like a thousand questions, Rose answered few of them and the answers she did give were mostly grunts and shrugs. Fresh girl, Mume thought again. She was glad Fanny wasn't like that!

Mume looked over her shoulder, but Rose was still in the girls' bedroom doing the mending. Mume tapped her foot impatiently and squinted hard through the window, as if she could pull Moshe home with strong wishes.

At last! There he was! Mume ran to the door of their flat and pulled it open. The sounds and smells of the other apartments in the tenement washed over her and she wrinkled her nose.

A mother on another floor shouted at her son: "Izzy, I'm baking! Stay out of the kitchen!"

A young girl called: "Mama! Can I make a hair ribbon out of this scrap?" and when her mama didn't answer, she screamed her question again.

Mume heard Moshe's heavy step on the stairs below and she yelled her own question down at him.

"So? Moshe? You found Rose a place?"

Moshe looked up tiredly, though he couldn't see her in the doorway yet. "I found, I found," he mumbled as he climbed slowly toward her. "The woman can't wait until I get upstairs, she has to yell our business all over the place, the whole world should know . . ."

"What?" Mume screamed at him.

"Wait, screaming woman, wait!" Moshe hollered and pushed his body up the final flight.

Mume was watching him, frowning. "Stamp the sawdust outside," she cautioned. "Brush it off your clothes—stay there! Brush."

38

Moshe stood in the doorway, wearily slapping at his clothes.

"Skloots will take Rose," he said. "She'll share a bed with Hinde. She'll work at Griffin Cap in the daytime and she'll do her sewing for Skloots at night. Everyone will be happy—will you now close your mouth?"

But Mume wasn't wasting a moment. "Rose!" she called. "Get your things! You're going to—"

"Wait, howling woman!" Moshe barked and held up his hand. "Tomorrow is soon enough. Tomorrow she'll go to Skloots's. Today she stays here. And she does no more work. She rests!"

"Rests!" Mume hissed. "Why should she rest? Do I rest? Do you? Why should she rest? Is she a king's daughter?"

"She can have one day," Moshe said quietly. "Listen to me, Mume . . . Lowenstein was bad to Rose. So she can have one day."

"How, bad? What, bad?"

"Bad, Mume, bad!" He sat down on one of the kitchen chairs. "After I left Skloots this morning, I saw him. Lowenstein. He was buying a hammer from Greskin. He saw me, he left right away without taking the hammer."

"So?"

"So, Mume, he already paid for the hammer. I saw him pay for the hammer. And he left without taking what he paid for. And he said nothing to me about Rose leaving him. Nothing to me, not even, 'How is it with you, Olshansky?' He's a guilty man, Mume. I thought so and I was right."

Mume twisted her lips together. "All right," she said

39

finally. "All right. But tomorrow morning she goes to Sklootes'!"

Leave-taking ‿

Rose stood in the kitchen, again holding her suitcase.

"I'm ready to go," she told Mume. "Is there anything you want me to do before I leave?"

Mume looked at her. She was a short child, but plump. And only eleven and a half. She would probably be fat soon. Mume prided herself on her own slimness. She thought Fanny would be slim, too.

Rose shifted her body. She knew she was being studied. She waited until Mume was ready to either use her or dismiss her.

"You can go," Mume said finally. "Zena is a good woman. Hinde likes her."

"I know," Rose said. "She told me." They all saw each other at the Neschvizers, the social-club meetings organized by immigrants from Neschviz, her village. Each town had its own club. Those from Neschviz met weekly at a hall on Clinton Street, as a way for families to keep in touch with one another. If they didn't see each other during the week, at least they had the Sunday get-togethers for catching up on the news.

Rose loved the Neschvizers for another reason. They gave her a chance to play the piano.

No one had taught Rose to play, but she'd always loved music. The women of her village had sung—

peasant folk songs, songs they had made up about their lives, songs from the taverns, songs from the cities, arias from the great operas, whose words they did not know but whose melodies were familiar—always music somewhere for those who wanted to listen. Rose wanted to listen.

When she'd first begun to come to the Neschvizers, she'd been drawn to the piano, the first ever at her disposal, and started to pick out the little tunes she knew, humming to herself in a soft soprano and trying to find notes and chords that seemed to go with the tunes. Soon there were three or four songs she could play and sing all the way through, and she slowly began to add the new American songs she heard in the streets to her repertoire. When Meyer discovered her gift, he quickly made her a part of the evening, and now it was hard to imagine the Sunday night meetings without her, even though there were always fiddlers, sawing and rocking and tapping their feet.

Thinking about the piano made Rose smile and Mume sniffed. What had the girl to smile about, anyway?

"You'll go to the Griffin with Hinde and Skloots's girls," Mume said, reminding Rose of her obligations.

Rose nodded agreement.

"So, go then," Mume said with a wave of her hand, and as Rose turned, she added, "Eli is a good man, Rose."

"I know."

"So you don't have to worry—"

"Thank you for letting me stay two nights," Rose said quickly and hurried out the door and down the three flights of stairs.

"Didn't Papa Tell You?" ⌒

"So, Rose, why did you leave Lowenstein?" Hinde asked as she helped Rose unpack her few belongings. They were in the bedroom that Hinde shared with Anna and Lillian.

Rose fidgeted. "I just wanted to," she said noncommittally. "It will be good to get out of the house in the daytime . . . and there's no factory work to go to on Saturday and Sunday . . ."

"They'd like for us to come in on Shabbos, though," Hinde said, frowning. "They're always behind at Griffin, always yelling at us to work faster, faster. They'll always squeeze in another sewing machine for a new worker . . . Pretty soon we'll be working on top of each other's heads—"

"I don't mind," Rose said quietly.

"Well, we work just as hard here on Saturdays and Sundays, though . . . Don't think they're holidays, Rose."

Rose looked up. "On Shabbos?"

"Who has time to keep Shabbos?" Hinde said with a shrug. "Oh, we light the candles Friday night . . . and Zena bakes . . . but who can sit in shul when there's so much to be done? We have to sew for Eli's cart on the weekends."

Rose shook her head.

"Didn't Papa tell you? That's why Eli was so glad to have you. Because you sew better and faster than anyone."

Rose wasn't sure if there was bitterness or amusement in Hinde's voice. But she had to smile at Moshe's not mentioning this extra work to her. Moshe's manipulations were exasperating, yet amusing all the same.

"Anyway," Hinde continued, "we have to make Eli's things. Blankets, quilts, doilies, afghans, shawls . . . you know."

"Yes . . ."

"It takes getting used to. Sewing is one thing, but sewing all the time is another. And, of course, there's still the housework we all have to share. You should have stayed where you were, Rose. I think Lowenstein spoiled you."

THREE

1896

An Announcement ⬱

The sewing machines were silent while the woman made her brief announcement, and the moment she was through, they all began to clatter again. Except Rose's.

"What's the matter, Rose?" Anna called to her across the aisle. "Are you all right?"

"Of course I am!" Rose answered, her cheeks bright with excitement. "Didn't you hear?"

"Hear what?"

"That lady! What she said!"

"Oh," Anna said, bewildered. "You mean about the night classes?"

"For learning to read and write English!" Rose said. "Isn't that wonderful? And the classes will be held right in the same public school that Celia and Fanny go to!"

"You want to go?" Anna asked. "What for?"

"Anna! 'What for!' I can learn to read and write English, Anna! I can learn to read American books!"

"Oh, Rose, when would you have the time to read books," Anna sighed and returned to her sewing.

"I'll always have time to read books," Rose said, her own work forgotten. "Oh, they meet tomorrow night! I don't think I can wait until then!"

She hardly managed to get much work done either until Mr. Warren, the foreman, threatened her and forced her to concentrate on her cap linings.

English Class

Rose and her fellow students, all immigrants like herself, were squeezed into school benches built for eight-year-olds, their knees reaching to and rubbing against the desks. But Rose didn't even notice.

"Why are you wasting your time, Rose?" Hinde had demanded that evening as Rose was leaving the Sklootses' flat. She licked her aching fingers and bent again over the pillowcase she was stitching. "There just isn't time for things that have no meaning in life, Rose."

"This has meaning for me, Hinde," Rose had replied firmly. "It has meaning in my life." Hinde, Lillian and fifteen-year-old Anna had shaken their heads as Rose swept out the door.

"Don't say anything to your papa, Hinde," Lillian warned, and Hinde rolled her eyes at the thought of Moshe's finding out about Rose at night classes.

Now, the young teacher, Mr. Pratt, was writing something on the blackboard at the front of the room. Rose leaned forward, as if staring harder would make her understand the strange lettering.

"It says 'English Class,' " the man next to her whispered.

"Does it? You can read it already?" Rose was astonished.

"Well," the man said, "it's logical, isn't it? That's what this is, that's what he'd write. 'English Class,' " he repeated.

The teacher turned around. "Do any of you speak English?" he asked. "Even a little?"

Almost everyone raised a hand. There were words one had to know in the new language, though most of their trading was done amongst themselves.

"Good!" The teacher turned to the board and the words he had written. "These words say 'Albert Pratt,' " he told the class.

" 'Albert Pratt'?" Rose repeated with a smile. "Not 'English Class'?" The man next to her looked away and coughed.

"My name," the young teacher continued, pointing to himself and then to the words on the blackboard. "Albert Pratt. Me. The first English words you will learn tonight—my name. This makes me feel— important." He flexed his muscles and strutted at the front of the room. Rose caught the gist of his words and laughed out loud. Mr. Pratt smiled at her and winked.

"I don't speak Yiddish," Mr. Pratt continued, "except for a few words. But you will learn from me, anyway, because I can act out anything you don't understand." The faces in front of him were confused. "Don't worry. You'll see. Now! The letter *A*."

Rose folded her hands on the little desk. She decided she liked this young man. Learning English would not be easy, but she would do it. She would do it well!

"This isn't for me," the man next to her muttered. "I don't have time for this."

Rose frowned at him.

Sunday Evening ➤

At thirteen, Lillian Skloots—despite her cramped flat, her hand-me-down clothes and her calloused fingers —daydreamed through work of love and marriage and put herself into all the lyrics of the popular songs. She knew that her sister Anna was terribly in love with Rose's brother, Meyer, and she married them off in her mind at least twice a day.

As she walked toward Clinton Street, zigzagging through the crowds, her mind pictured Anna in a wedding gown made of white satin with a long train and Meyer in a beautiful black suit, holding his bride as they waltzed by themselves in the middle of the floor. But she was jerked back into reality by a voice calling her name.

"Lillian! Where are you?"

It was Rose—far ahead of Lillian—way up the street. In her daydream, Lillian had fallen behind and Rose had apparently not noticed until now.

Hurrying back, Rose was chattering at her: "—and

I was talking to myself for a whole block before I knew you were gone! So embarrassed! What happened to you, Lillian? Dreaming again?"

"Oh, Rose . . . I'm sorry. Yes, I was dreaming . . ." She hugged a box containing a Skloots family speciality—a sponge cake—to share with their neighbors.

"What was it this time? Your wedding? Or Anna's?" Rose was grinning.

They were on their way to the weekly Neschvizer.

"We should slow down, anyway," Lillian said in an attempt to change the subject. "Mama and Papa and Hinde and Anna are way behind us. What's your hurry? It's only Neschvizer. Everyone will make you work all night."

Rose laughed. "It isn't work, making music. It's fun."

"You know, Rose," Lillian said, "if I weren't so tired all the time, I'd be tired just from watching you. You do more work than any of us and then you run out most nights. I don't know how you do it. Or why, Rose."

"I just want to," Rose said.

Lillian shook her head. When Rose had come to stay with the Sklootses a year ago, she had tried hard to become friendly with Hinde's and Meyer's little sister. But Rose had been so quiet and so closed-in. Lillian couldn't break through. Rose had certainly done her share of the work and more besides, but she wouldn't talk or laugh—or dream with Lillian. Now things were different. It was as if Rose had shrugged off the burden she'd been carrying. She sang, laughed— she was a terrible tease. And while Lillian still missed

48

someone to dream with, she felt a new kinship with this landsman of her own age, this boarder in her home, Rose Olshansky.

They had almost arrived at the hall. Lillian took Rose's arm.

"You're different now, Rose," she said in a burst of confession. "And I'm glad!" But she went on before Rose could reply: "I love all the energy you have and the way we can laugh at the same things—and I love the way you sing . . ."

"Well . . . I'm happy with your family, Lillian," Rose told her. "I even like working at Griffin."

"How can you possibly like working at Griffin!" Lillian drew back. "It's terrible there! Hot in the summer, freezing in the winter . . . Mr. Warren . . . ugh!"

"Yes, that's all true," Rose agreed, "but it's because of the factory that I found out I could go to school. If I were in a private house, no one would have told me. I still wouldn't know there was a night school for us."

"For *you*," Lillian said. "Not me. No one understands why you're so interested in that, anyway. None of us cares about it at all."

"Well, I do," Rose said and laughed. "Now come on, little dreamer. Walk a little faster!"

Neschvizer ⌁

"Is that you, Meyer Olshansky, you handsome boy?"

Meyer, standing near the door at the Clinton Street

hall, jumped at the sound of his name. He'd been
sneaking glances toward the entrance, waiting for Anna
Skloots to arrive so that his evening could begin.

"It *is* you, Meyer! Will you dance a dance with me
tonight?"

Meyer smiled broadly at the heavy woman in black
who was greeting him.

"Of course, Mrs. Wolf!" he cried. "I would be happy
to!"

"But only if your sister Rose plays the piano," Mrs.
Wolf said. "Only Rose plays the happiest dancing music and the saddest singing music . . ."

"She learned all by herself," Meyer said proudly.

"But will you dance with me even if the Skloots girl
comes?" Mrs. Wolf teased. "Even then, Meyer Olshansky?"

"Even then, Mrs. Wolf."

"Your father raised a good son. He'll be here tonight? With Mume? And Fanny and Celia?"

"Maybe," Meyer said. He rarely talked to his father
during the week, but at the Neschvizers, Moshe spent
much time kissing him and slapping him hard on the
back—sometimes so hard that Meyer would cough.
But the harder the slap, the more affectionate the
display, according to Moshe.

"And Yette?" Mrs. Wolf continued. She was a widow,
who lived with her daughter's family and spent most
of her time paying attention to all the families of her
landsmen. "Will Yette come? Will the Resniks?"

"Yette—maybe not. Mrs. Resnik may not be feeling
well enough . . ." Mrs. Resnik had had another child
the month before. She had barely recovered from the

earlier one. Now there were five Resnik children and Yette had her hands full. Meyer heard the news from Mr. Resnik, whose grocery store Meyer frequented.

"Oy, poor woman," Mrs. Wolf said, slapping the side of her cheek. "So Resnik's running the store himself. And Yette has all those children, such a young girl. It's no good, a man alone with all those children."

"Well, Mrs. Resnik is there," Meyer said, "but she can't—"

"No good," Mrs. Wolf interrupted. "A man alone. I'll see you later, Meyer. You said you'd dance with me, remember."

Meyer smiled to himself as she walked away. Mrs. Wolf loved gossip, but she always heard what she wanted to hear, which wasn't always what was actually told to her.

He glanced again toward the front door. Would Anna ever get here? The fiddlers had started and the hall had begun to be thick with the smell of pumpernickel and herring and cake and ripe fruit, as friends and family from their little Russian village gathered to be together for an evening of fun: of remembering—and forgetting.

The door opened and there was a burst of laughter. Meyer peered hopefully through the small group of new arrivals and his face lit up as he recognized Lillian Skloots and his sister Rose. He hurried over to them.

"Rosele!" he cried as he kissed her. "And Lillian! We've been waiting for you!"

"For us? For us, Meyer?" Lillian teased.

Meyer blushed. He had been about to ask casually where the rest of the Sklootses were and now, from embarrassment, he couldn't. But Lillian didn't have the heart to keep him in suspense.

"She's coming, Meyer. She's not far behind us."

Meyer nodded, but couldn't hide his smile. He turned to his sister.

"Everyone has been waiting for your music," he told her. "Everyone wants to sing and dance."

"Oh, let her catch her breath, Meyer," Lillian said. "She just got here. Come, Rose, let's go put the sponge cake on the table."

"Oh, good!" Meyer cried. "Mama Zena's sponge cake! The party wouldn't be complete without it."

"I agree," Lillian said, "but this week I made it. Mama was by Resniks' all week, helping with the new baby. It's a little boy, in case you haven't heard."

"I heard. Mr. Resnik told me. I'm glad Yette wasn't alone there with the children."

"Oh, no. Someone had to be there so Yette could go the factory. At night, Yette took over and Mama came home. Yette's there now, though. She probably won't be able to get out on weekends until Mrs. Resnik is better."

But Meyer was looking over Lillian's shoulder. "Ah! Here comes Anna!" he cried. "And the others."

Rose slipped past them into the crowded room.

"Good, good! Rose Olshansky is here!" someone called. "Rose is here, everyone! The dancing begins!"

Rose was ushered to where the piano stood near a small platform that was used as a stage. Laughing, she sat down on the bench and flexed her fingers.

"Ah, Rose Olshansky!" Schmuel Cohen beamed. "Come on, Rose, I want to hear my favorite American song! You can play it, you know—'Dais-y, Dais-y, da da da da-aa da da—' How does it go?"

" 'I'm so craz-y, all for the love of you-ou-ou,' " someone sang, and soon others had joined in. Rose's voice could be heard clearly above the rest:

> *It won't be a sty-lish marriage;*
> *I can't af-ford a carriage;*
> *But you'll look sweet*
> *Upon the seat*
> *Of a bi-cycle built for two-ooo-ooo!*

"Ahhhh!" the crowd murmured appreciatively, and then, "More, Rose, more! A polka for dancing!"

"She hasn't had anything to eat yet," Lillian chided. "Here's a glass of Seltzer, Rose. And a sweet roll—Mrs. Cohen's own!" Rose took a big gulp of Seltzer from the glass Lillian handed her. There was never a meal served without the effervescent mineral water, except perhaps breakfast. And everyone drank Seltzer to relieve thirst.

Stout, full-faced Mrs. Wolf bustled up to Rose and Lillian.

"I hear Mrs. Resnik died with this last child, Lillian," she sighed. "So fast it came after her fourth. No wonder."

"Oh, no, Mrs. Wolf. She didn't die. She's very sick, though. Mama's been there helping."

"So, Rose," Mrs. Wolf said, "now Yette will stay home from the factory and take care of the Resnik children?"

"Well, I don't know, Mrs. Wolf," Rose answered. "I

haven't talked to Yette since the baby came. But maybe she will . . . for a while . . ."

"What else can she do?" Mrs. Wolf wailed. "For a while . . . How long is 'a while' with poor Mrs. Resnik dead, may she rest in peace. Till Resnik gets married again? Maybe he'll marry Yette now, Rose?"

"Mrs. Resnik isn't dead, Mrs. Wolf," Lillian repeated. "She isn't dead. She's alive. Yette's only helping while she's sick!"

But Mrs. Wolf was holding her head with both hands.

"Oy, poor Resnik," Mrs. Wolf moaned. "He's lucky Yette is there. Such good girls, the Olshanskys. They had the funeral already?"

Rose pressed her lips together to keep from laughing, while Lillian kept patiently explaining that Mrs. Resnik had not died.

"Oy, oy," Mrs. Wolf continued to sigh. "Five children—it's five, right? I thought I kept count—five poor children . . . It's hard without a mother, believe me, I know. My own mother, may she rest in peace, died in childbirth . . . I never knew her, but to this day, I miss her. Oy! So, Lillian, the funeral?"

Lillian looked helplessly at Rose.

"Yes, it's all over, Mrs. Wolf," Rose said, folding her arms and lowering her head. "It was very nice. Yette brought the baby."

Mrs. Wolf sighed contentedly. "Good," she said, "The baby should be there." And she turned away, nodding to herself.

Lillian grinned at Rose. "What a thing to tell her, Rose!" she said, shaking her head.

"I had to!" Rose laughed. "Mrs. Wolf can do her mourning now, just as she planned, and Mrs. Resnik can still be alive. Everybody's happy! Come on now, Lillian—let's hear the rest of the gossip before they sit me down at the piano again."

As they moved around the room, greeting relatives and neighbors, Lillian leaned over and whispered to Rose, "I think the gossip's all about you!"

"Me? What could they say about me?"

"They're talking about your night school," Lillian told her. "Didn't you hear? We passed that group over there with the Cohens and the Scheppers and Mr. Goldman—and as soon as we came near they stopped their buzz-buzzing and talked very loudly about something else."

"So, Lillian?"

"So, I know when people do that. So I dawdled a little. And as soon as they thought we were gone, they started again. Mrs. Schepper pointed at you and she said 'school.' I heard 'school.' "

"Maybe they think it's a good thing," Rose said.

"You know better. They think you're crazy."

Rose helped herself to a date-filled cookie and another glass of Seltzer. "Well, I don't care at all what they think," she said. "I'm going to read and write English words. And I'm going to learn how to do numbers. And you know what else?"

"No, what?" Lillian's mouth was open.

"I'm going to learn to play the piano right! I'm going to learn how to read the music! Maybe I'll even learn to play the violin . . . I love the violin, Lillian . . .

And I'm going to learn all the words to *The Barber of Seville!*"

Lillian burst into laughter. "Rose, you are so funny!" she cried. "*The Barber of Seville!* Wait till I tell Anna!"

"Tell Anna what?" Meyer suddenly appeared with Lillian's sister at his side. "What did Rose say that was so funny?"

But from the look on Rose's face, Lillian wasn't sure now if she'd been joking. "Oh . . ." she said, "it probably wouldn't seem so funny now . . . It was just something about . . . school . . ." Her voice trailed.

"School! Yes, Anna told me you'd signed up, Rosele. I'm proud of you! I think it's a good thing!"

Rose's face relaxed. "Thank you, Meyer. You seem to be the only one who thinks so."

"Ah, well, we'll keep it from Papa, then, won't we?"

"We'd better!"

Meyer laughed. "Yes, I think we'd better. But won't you be too tired, Rosele? You'll still have to do all your share for Eli besides the factory. And the factory's twelve hours a day, Rose!"

"Meyer, I know what I have to do. And I don't get tired easily. I have a lot of energy, Meyer, and I want to do things."

"But why?" Anna asked. "What for?"

But Rose only shrugged. "I don't know, Anna. I just need to."

Anna shook her head uncomprehendingly. "We just need to learn to be good mothers and wives," she said. She glanced at Meyer through her eyelashes and blushed.

"Oh, look!" Lillian cried, pointing. "Over there!"

Anna turned. "Where? There? You mean Mr. Lowenstein?"

"Mr. Lowenstein!" Rose frowned and caught her lower lip between her teeth. The Lowensteins had pointedly stayed away from Neschvizer ever since Rose left their flat.

"That's not Lowenstein," Meyer said, craning his neck. "It's a much younger man. He's a stranger." Rose sighed with relief.

"A good-looking stranger," Anna said.

"No, he's not," Meyer said quickly. "You need glasses, Anna. You thought he was Lowenstein, now you think he's good-looking!"

"Never mind who he is or what he looks like!" Lillian said, smiling. "Look who he's talking to!"

Meyer, Anna and Rose all followed Lillian's gaze.

"Oh, it's Hinde!" Rose breathed. Tall Hinde was looking into the stranger's face. And she was laughing!

"Look! She's laughing! Hinde is laughing!" Anna cried, covering her mouth with her fingers. "I never saw Hinde laugh out loud before, did you?"

"This must be serious," Meyer said. "Hinde laughing? The family sourpuss? I think we'd better get her dowry ready."

"But who is it?" Lillian persisted. "Does anyone know?"

"Let's find out," Rose said, pulling at Lillian's sleeve. "Mrs. Wolf knows everything. Let's ask her!"

"Not Mrs. Wolf!" Lillian groaned. "She only says what she believes, not what's true!"

"But she'll know who he is! Come on!"

Hinde and Jacov ⌒

Hinde took her eyes from the young man's face. It was nice, she thought, to be able to look up at a man. She was so tall, it seemed as though she was always looking down. Her happy smile faded. She wanted to say something impressive to this newcomer with the neatly trimmed beard, but she wasn't sure how to begin.

"Well . . ." she said hesitantly, "let me see if I understand. You are boarding with the Goldmans . . . but you are an Abramson. Your father—"

"My father was Isadore Abramson, brother to Letty Goldman. You remember the Abramsons from the dairy, Miss Olshansky?"

Hinde nodded. "Oh, yes," she said, "but I don't remember *you*, Mr. Abramson . . ."

He smiled. "I'm not surprised. I'm older than you are but I was always very small for my age. And shy. I used to watch you and your sisters when I was helping my father. You always walked so straight—with your head high—I thought you looked like someone regal."

Hinde blushed. "Well . . . you . . ." she stammered, "you aren't small for your age anymore."

"Oh, no," he laughed. "Not anymore. I seemed to grow overnight. I amazed myself!"

Hinde laughed. He didn't talk the way other men did. "And," she said, "you don't seem so shy anymore, either."

"I'm not," he agreed. "I got over that on the boat. I was traveling alone and I was one of the lucky ones. I didn't get sick."

"Oh, you *were* lucky. I thought I would die on that boat. And I felt so awful because I was the oldest and in charge. I thought I should be taking care of the others. But Meyer and Yette seemed to be all right. Rose and Celia were as ill as I was." Hinde took a breath. She was talking more than she ever had to anyone, much less a stranger and a man!

But the young man didn't seem to notice. He was shaking his head. "I know," he was saying. His face turned grim. "May we never know anything like that again. One basin we had . . . it was the dishpan for greasy tins, it was the laundry tub for dirty handkerchiefs and clothing, it was the bowl for shampoos—without any special cleaning. And it was the only bowl available for seasickness . . ."

"No, please," Hinde said softly. "Let's not remember."

He was instantly apologetic. "Of course! I'm so sorry—It's only . . . it's only that it's still so much with me. I've only just arrived, you see."

"I know that. I'm sorry, too. It was the same with me when I first came. It took months before I didn't think of that voyage the minute I opened my eyes in the morning. Of course it's still with you, Mr. Abramson."

They continued to talk, calling each other "Miss Olshansky" and "Mr. Abramson" until he asked if he might use her first name, if she would call him Jacov. He told her of his father's and sister's deaths of the "coughing disease"; of the deaths of his two cows and the destruction of his business and of the market-place.

"The Cossacks rode in with torches—they set fire to everything."

"I know," Hinde said. She had seen her share of pogroms.

"One threw a rock into the window of our little cottage . . . It struck my baby sister on the head. She was sleeping in her cradle."

Hinde closed her eyes.

"Everyone left after that last pogrom," Jacov sighed. "It was time to leave, so everyone left. Neschviz is no more, our little village." And then his face changed. "And now look! Here is everyone who left! All together again in this new country! I'm glad we meet here, Hinde. Instead of at the dairy in the village." He smiled and glanced away and Hinde caught for the first time a glimpse of his old shyness.

"I'm glad, too, Jacov," she said.

"Hello, Hinde," a small voice piped and Hinde, startled, looked down to find her sister Rose with Lillian Skloots.

"Oh," Hinde said and took a small step away from Jacov Abramson. "Rose. Mr. Abramson—this is—"

"This is Rose Olshansky," Rose said with a grin. "Hinde's sister. And this is Lillian Skloots, perhaps you remember her father, Eli. He was a tailor in Neschviz, and here he makes—"

"Rose, Rose!" Hinde interrupted and glanced at Jacov. "A little slower, Rose, please, Mr. Abramson's only just arrived. He will meet everyone soon enough . . ."

But Jacov Abramson bowed deeply and took Rose's and Lillian's hands.

"I'm proud and happy to meet such lovely ladies," he said and Lillian giggled. "My name is—"

"Oh, we know," Lillian said quickly. "Your name is Jules Abramson, your father had a dairy, you're Letty Goldman's nephew and Edna Goldman's cousin and you got here two days ago."

"Everything is correct," Jacov said with a broad smile, "but it's Jacov, not Jules. And I was right—it's just like the old country, with news traveling as quickly as it is made! Everyone knows everything immediately!"

"It's nice to meet you, Mr. Abramson," Rose said politely.

"Rose, why don't you show Mr. Abramson how well you play the piano?" Hinde said pointedly.

Rose's eyes twinkled. "All right," she said, and whispered, "if you want to get rid of me."

"I liked you better when you didn't talk so much," Hinde snapped.

"Rose, the things you say!" Lillian scolded as they walked away.

"Hinde's face was so red," Rose laughed. "She likes that man. He's very tall, isn't he? At last, someone taller than Hinde!"

Lillian sighed. "So, a nice match, maybe," she said. Here was another couple for her to dream about. The new arrival, Jacov Abramson, and her very own roommate, Hinde Olshansky.

Rose helped herself to a handful of nuts and raisins from a small chipped dish. "Maybe," she agreed, and she spoke some of Lillian's dreams aloud. "Hinde and

the Abramson cousin . . . Meyer and your sister, Anna
. . . Soon everyone will be married. Except me."

"Why not you?"

"Oh, I'm too strange. And too fat. And I don't care,
anyway." She poured herself more Seltzer.

"Of course you care," Lillian said. "And you will get
married. We all will. Everyone gets married."

"What's Family For?"

That night, Rose lay awake in bed. Hinde was next
to her, snoring loudly. The two Skloots girls were
sound asleep, too.

Rose felt something strange in her stomach. They
started as small cramps, but soon had her doubled
up, with her knees touching her chin. She felt trickles
of perspiration behind her ears and down her neck.
Her whole face felt hot.

It will go away, she thought. It will go away. Don't
wake anyone.

But it didn't go away and it suddenly seemed as if
she were blowing up. Her legs felt swollen, her stomach and her arms—

She moaned.

Hinde rolled over and flung her arm across Rose's
waist.

"Hinde . . ." Rose said softly. "Hinde, wake up . . ."

"Hm," Hinde grunted.

"Hinde, please . . ."

"Mmm? What?"

Rose poked her. "Hinde, I'm dying," she said.

"Dying?"

"I'm dying," Rose repeated. "I wanted to tell you, so it's not a shock when you wake up." Her whole body felt hot and tight, as if she were about to burst. She began to cry softly.

Hinde, awake now, touched Rose's arm. She drew back with a gasp.

"Rose, you're burning!" she cried. "Anna! Lillian! Zena! Eli! Everyone wake up! Rose is dying!"

The household sprang into activity. Zena Skloots, tired as she was from the added responsibilities of the Resnik family, was the first at Rose's bedside.

"She's burning up!" Zena gasped.

"I told you, I told you!" Hinde cried.

Rose was in too much pain to feel shame and embarrassment at the attention. Zena was putting cold cloths on her head and neck; Lillian was holding and squeezing her hand while crying softly; Anna brought a pan of ice water for Rose to put her feet in; Hinde fluttered about like a distraught bird; and Eli ran down the tenement stairs into the street, calling, "A doctor! A doctor! My child is dying! A doctor!"

"You hear him out there, Rose?" Lillian said. Tears were streaming down her cheeks. "You hear Papa? He said 'my child.' He's calling for a doctor and naming you as his child. We love you, Rose . . ."

Rose would have smiled if she hadn't felt like a firecracker about to explode. Eli was calling her his child because she was dying. The more he showed he loved Rose, the more bereft he felt at her death, the more sympathy and attention he'd get at her funeral. Rose knew it and she didn't blame him. He deserved consideration; he had taken her in and given her a home. He'd barely spoken to her in the year she'd lived with him and his family and Rose would have been surprised if he'd known her name. But in death, she could be his daughter and everyone would cry with him. He deserved it—good Eli. His voice reached them from the street below.

"—Doctor! Doctor! Someone!"

"He'll find someone, Rose," Zena said.

"You won't die, you won't . . ." Lillian sobbed.

Lillian, Rose knew, did love her as a sister and she hoped Lillian wouldn't mourn too long after she was gone.

There was a pounding on the stairs.

"Eli's back!" Zena said and went to meet him.

"Lillian . . ." Rose whispered and Lillian bent down to hear better. "My shawl . . . the one I made."

"Do you want it, Rose?"

But Rose shook her head impatiently. "No, no. You. I want you to have it. I'm going to die any minute."

"No, no, no!" Lillian wailed and fresh tears spilled down her cheeks and soaked into her cotton nightgown.

"Here's Dr. Ziff. It's Dr. Ziff," Zena said, hurrying back into the room. "Eli got Dr. Ziff from First Avenue. Get out of the way, Lillian, move Hinde. Here, Doctor . . . Here she is . . . Look at her face, it's like the moon it's so round . . ."

The doctor peered at Rose.

"I'm dying," Rose said.

Dr. Ziff grunted. He touched Rose's head, arms, feet. He looked inside her mouth. He listened to her heart. Then he grunted again. Around the bed the Sklootses and Hinde clustered, wringing their hands.

"No, no. She's not dying," Dr. Ziff said. He took a small envelope out of his bulging pocket and handed it to Rose. "You take this. You'll feel better. Swelling will go down."

Rose looked at the packet. "What's in it?"

"Doesn't matter," the doctor said. "It will make you go. You go, you feel better."

"I'm not dying?" Rose looked up, the pain forgotten momentarily.

"Not dying."

"Not dying?" Eli asked from the doorway.

"Not dying."

Lillian slid to the floor next to Rose's bed. "Thank God," she said and sobbed loudly.

"So, Doctor, what does she have?" Zena said, following him out. And she added softly, "Can we all get it?"

"I'll tell you what she needs to do," the doctor said, loudly enough to be heard by everyone. "The Seltzer she can cut down on, the fats she can cut down on. She does that, it won't come back. She swelled up from the Seltzer, her body didn't get rid of it. Maybe your bodies hold in the liquid, too. Watch how much you drink." And he left.

"So she's not dying." Eli was shaking his head at the door.

"Thank God," Lillian whispered.

"I'm sorry I woke you all up," Rose said in a tiny voice. "I thought everything was over."

"Oh, Rose," Anna said, touching her knee, "what's family for?"

Still clutching her stomach as she lay in the bed, Rose had to smile to herself. She had three sisters and a brother, a father, a stepmother and a stepsister, but she knew her family extended even beyond them. All of these landsmen, these countrymen so far from home, all of these survivors were her family, too.

The pain was still bad enough to cause tears but Rose knew now that she would not die.

"Lillian?" she said.

"I'm here, Rose, I'm here . . ."

"The pain will be gone by tomorrow the doctor said?"

"Soon. After you take the medicine."

"Good," Rose said. "Then I won't have to miss school."

FOUR

1897

Stirrings ⌁

It had begun to snow and on the jammed streets the pure white flakes were already turning into muddy slush. The vendors at their pushcarts—their breaths steamy over their wares—pulled their cloth coats, shawls and other makeshift wraps tighter around their bodies and stamped their feet to keep warm.

Celia elbowed her way through the crowd. Her hands were stuffed into the pockets of her "new" old coat, bought by Yette for fifty cents at one of the carts. The coat was much too big for her, but it was better than wearing Fanny's old one which was too small. Celia was concentrating on her school lesson, her "gazin-tas," as she called them.

"Four gazinta eight two times, six gazinta twelve two times, eight gazinta sixteen two times," she recited to herself until she felt two hands grab her shoulders from behind. She whirled around and looked up into the laughing face of her sister Rose.

"What were you mumbling to yourself?" Rose asked. She pulled at Celia's extra-large coat. "You look like a little rabbi mumbling his prayers on his way home from shul."

"I was saying my lessons," Celia answered. "Numbers. They're easy. And I can read, too, Rose!"

"I can, too. Isn't it wonderful? Tell me, Celiale, why haven't you been to Neschvizer lately? I haven't seen you in weeks."

"Mume has so much for me to do," Celia answered. "I don't have much time for play. But Fanny goes. Haven't you seen her? I'm on my way to school. Fanny's not going today, she stayed in bed. Is Hinde really going to get married? Papa speaks in whispers about it, but somehow Fanny and I hear all the news—"

"Stop! You sound like Lillian! Marriage, marriage! That's all anyone talks about! But, yes, Hinde and Jacov are very serious—he comes each night to walk her out—he's very nice. Celia, I must go. I'm late for work. But tell me—are you well?"

"Very well." She reached up and hugged her sister. "Give my love to Hinde. Tell her I can't wait to see her as a bride!"

"Celia, you come to Neschvizer Sunday. Bring Mume's work with you and I'll help you with it. And I'll bring you some shoes. You need better shoes."

Celia hurried off with a wave, leaving Rose to frown at the ripped seams in her sister's high-topped boots.

With a shake of her head, Rose turned away and continued to walk briskly. She was late for work at the Griffin Cap Factory and she knew she'd have to double her piecework so as not to lose her desperately needed pay. The women took home $1.50 a week and the Sklootses and her father depended on her for their shares of it. But today Rose was tired. She had stayed up very late, after helping Zena and the others with a set of lace doilies, because there was a book she wanted to read. It was called *The Prince and the Pauper* by an American, Mark Twain. Mr. Pratt had given it to her because he said he thought she would enjoy it.

Mr. Pratt had singled Rose out at the very first class because she seemed to catch on so quickly. He was from "uptown"—somewhere way above Fourteenth Street. It may as well have been the moon to Rose: neither she nor anyone she knew had seen anything of New York City but the Lower East Side.

Mr. Pratt was a university student who volunteered his time to teach English to the poor immigrants. After the first lesson, all but ten students had dropped out and now there were only six left. Rose thought Mr. Pratt would be discouraged, but he never seemed so. He never missed a class, and it was easier to learn with so few in the group. Mr. Pratt had told Rose he was proud of her and he made her feel proud, too, so she tried very hard to read *The Prince and the Pauper*. She pronounced each word to herself, moving her lips as she read, but there were so many difficult words and phrases that Rose had fallen asleep exhausted over the book and, this morning, hadn't risen when

Zena called, "Up!" Hinde, Anna and Lillian had left without her and now she was late. In her worry about it, she hardly felt the cold.

She reached the big wooden door of the factory and slipped quickly inside, stamping the snow off her feet. She didn't see the manager, Mr. Warren, moving catlike down the rickety stairs.

"What happened to you this morning, Miss Olshanksy?" he asked stiffly.

Rose jumped. "Oh! Mr. Warren—I'm sorry—I—"

"Don't waste any more time explaining. Get to your machine, before you're docked."

Nodding, Rose hurried up the three flights. Why didn't he dock me right then? she wondered. It's not like him at all not to scream and take a dime away from me . . . He was almost—nice!

The clatter of a hundred sewing machines greeted Rose in the airless loft above. No one looked up to greet her—it would mean a loss of time. Quietly, she slid into her chair and reached for the pile of caps to be lined on her table. But she'd barely started when she felt a nudge at her shoulder.

"Miss Olshansky?"

"Yes . . ."

"My name is Isadore Mestrovich. I work—" he raised his eyes—"on the floor above."

"I—I can't waste time, Mr. Mestrovich," Rose said, bending over her work again. "I was late this morning—"

"I know, I know—I've talked to the others and I must be quick, too, before I'm caught. We want to unionize Griffin, Miss Olshansky. We're working to unionize this factory. Do you know what that means?"

"Union-ize?"

"Quickly it means we all unite—as one—to stop some of the terrible conditions under which we work. You know what those are, Miss Olshansky—may I call you Rose?"

Rose nodded and finished her seam.

"Rose, then. If we all stick together, all threaten to leave together if things are not made better, Warren and Mr. Griffin and the others will have to listen to us. Because we will all be together, not talking as individuals they could easily fire and replace. Do you see?"

Rose looked up and frowned. "I'm not . . . sure," she said.

"What are you doing on this floor, Mestrovich!" came a voice from across the room. The machines went silent, but only for a moment. The clatter began again and everyone turned away as Mr. Warren came striding toward Rose.

"I am Miss Olshansky's cousin," Isadore Mestrovich said slowly in broken English. "I wished to know the— the state of my mother's health. Miss Olshansky was late this morning because she was caring for my poor mother."

Rose's mouth opened and closed.

"Is that true, Miss Olshansky?" Mr. Warren demanded.

Isadore Mestrovich was looking at her pleadingly.

"Yes," Rose said, lowering her eyelids, "and I had

no time to tell him that his mother is stronger and should be up again by lunch time."

Relief flooded Isadore Mestrovich's face. "Thank you—Rose," he said, giving her a small bow. "Thank you. I am happy to hear it."

"You're welcome." Rose's foot worked the machine's pedal. She did not look up at Mr. Warren, who turned away with a snort.

When he was gone, the girl working at the next machine spoke to Rose out of the side of her mouth.

"Be careful, Rose. Mestrovich is a troublemaker. He'll get us all fired if we listen to him."

Anna looked up from her work. "She's right, Rose, don't listen to him. Lillian and Hinde said he was on their floor yesterday, stirring up trouble."

"What is it, this 'unionize'?" Rose asked. "What did he mean?"

"He says we all join together, like a big club," Rose's workmate explained. "And we have a leader. Him, I guess! And the leader tells Mr. Warren all the bad things we have to put up with and that we will all strike if he doesn't make them better."

"Strike?"

"Walk around outside, carrying signs that say Griffin is not fair to its workers. It's crazy, Rose! Walk around outside in the cold when we should be in here earning money!"

"Miss Kushner?" Mr. Warren's voice boomed.

Miss Kushner turned beet red and moved her foot pedal faster. "Just be careful," she hissed at Rose without moving her lips.

Rose shook her head. There were so many new

words in this country . . . "unionize," "strike" . . . and all the words in *The Prince and the Pauper*! Would there ever be time to learn them all?

And then she had to make her mind a blank so she could double her output of piecework for this strange and shortened day.

A Common Cause ⟿

Isadore Mestrovich could still feel his knees shaking as he climbed the stairs to his own floor. If Rose Olshansky hadn't backed up his story, Mr. Warren would have thrown him out, fired him on the spot. And not only would he lose his much-needed job, but also the opportunity to make a change in it.

He was almost twenty years old. He had come to America with his mother and older sister in 1890 when he was twelve. His mother had died shortly afterward and his sister, a month later. Now he lived by himself in a coal cellar on Ludlow Street, and toiled by day doing piecework at Griffin Cap. He and some of his friends had been meeting and talking for months about forming a strong union—not like the small ones that had sprung up for buttonholemakers or liners or pocketmakers—but one big organization that included everyone—all garment workers.

It was a difficult task. The pressure from the bosses against unions was intolerable. The women were afraid and most of them were girls who felt they would soon marry and wouldn't need a union. But Mestrovich and his friends were determined that the union's day had come. So they stole precious time from their work and dared to approach others in their factories, trying to persuade them to join their common cause. After work, he and Hyman and Itzik and others would sit over Seltzer or tea or beer and argue and harangue each other well into the night.

Mestrovich sat down on a stool with a sigh. He picked up a pile of material from the floor. The dyes from the cloth had already blackened his fingers from his morning's labor and by tonight his hands would look as if he were wearing dark gloves.

A Sense of Duty ～

Yette hurried past the pushcarts and their owners yelling "Notebooks!" "Eyeglasses!" "Bananas!" "Socks!" "Pots!" and all the other bits of everyday life that everyone needed. She had bought what *she* needed, which was a pair of sharp scissors from her brother and Mr. Lister, some shoes and a wool cap so that the youngest Resnik would be able to go outside. The other children's hand-me-downs had been too worn even to mend.

Yette had had to quit her job at the shirtwaist factory. Mrs. Resnik had recovered sufficiently to help her husband part time in the grocery store, but not enough to manage the household of five children, two of whom were still under two years old.

Yette almost laughed aloud as she hurried along, thinking of the first time Mrs. Resnik appeared for work at the store after her long recuperation.

FOUR · 1897

The store was quiet and Mrs. Resnik had just settled herself on a padded stool behind the counter, when Mrs. Wolf came in for some "damaged" eggs. The woman had picked up two eggs and was shaking both of them next to her ears when she saw the pale Mrs. Resnik watching her.

"*Oy, Gott!*" Mrs. Wolf had screamed, dropped both eggs and hurried out of the store, still yelling.

Mrs. Resnik, her mouth open, gaped after her in astonishment.

"So what's with Mrs. Wolf?" Mr. Resnik had asked. He, too, was staring at the door Mrs. Wolf had hurtled herself through.

"I should know?" his wife answered. "She looked like she'd seen a ghost!"

Mrs. Wolf learned the truth, which was that Mrs. Resnik was still quite alive, from the owner of the dry-goods store into which she'd staggered and where she'd leaned against the wall, fanning her face with both hands.

"Oy, she didn't die," Mrs. Wolf kept repeating over and over. "Oy, she didn't die, thank God."

Yette smiled now, remembering how she and the Resniks had laughed at that episode. Poor Mrs. Wolf—she had almost died herself of a heart attack at the sight of the landsman she'd thought dead for months!

But now, rushing home with her purchases in a string bag, Yette still worried about Mrs. Resnik whom she could often hear in the night, moaning in pain.

"Yette, Yette—what's your hurry?" a voice at her elbow asked and Yette looked up, startled, into her sister Hinde's face. Hinde laughed. "You remind me

75

of that goat we used to keep back in the village, remember? She used to put down her head and butt all the other animals out of the way to get to her food!"

"Hinde—" Yette began. She felt jarred from her sense of purpose and duty. "Why aren't you at Griffin? Shouldn't you be at work this time of day?"

Hinde nodded. "I should. But I left for just a little while. There was some ribbon—something I wanted— needed for—" Hinde blushed, surprising her sister. "Anyway, I'm on my way back now. How is Mrs. Resnik? Oh—it's late—I really must go. Nice to see you, Yette—"

Yette frowned. Was that really Hinde? Laughing, blushing—and leaving work in the middle of the day! How Hinde normally would have scolded if the other members of the family behaved like that. This country seemed to change everyone!

Yette reached home, collected the babies from the neighbor who minded them and carried them both upstairs to their flat.

"Yet-te," Mrs. Resnik called weakly.

"Yes—it's me—I'm back," Yette answered. "Are you all right?"

"Can you come in a minute?" Mrs. Resnik asked.

Yette put the children down on a pile of rags in the corner of the kitchen. "Play nice," she told them. "I'll be right back." She hurried to the bedroom and repeated her question.

Mrs. Resnik said, "I'm all right. Mrs. Landau, the butcher's wife, was here."

"Yes?"

"She tells me it's definite your sister and the Abram-

76

son cousin are getting married. Why didn't you tell me?"

"Perhaps people are rushing Hinde and Jacov along faster than they may want to go," Yette said stiffly.

But Mrs. Resnik waved her hand. "No," she said. "I don't get out much but I feel things. There will be a wedding soon. And you, Yette, you must go to this wedding and there you will meet a husband of your own."

"And what will I do with this husband of my own?" Yette asked. "Will I bring him here to make you more crowded, Mrs. Resnik?"

Tears filled the older woman's eyes as she nodded her head. "If you have to. We will manage. You must have a life of your own, Yette."

Yette moved to the bed and took Mrs. Resnik's limp hand in hers. She pictured Hinde's face, laughing as it had been, earlier. She desperately longed for "a life of her own," but there was no prospective husband on the horizon; her papa had placed her with the Resniks and she felt obligated to all of them.

"I'm still young," she said, "and there's plenty of time. Maybe I'll think about it when the baby is finally in school and by that time you'll be stronger and back on your feet. Until that happens . . ." Yette took a breath . . . "I won't leave."

"Tonight!" ⬅

That same night, the Abramson cousin came to the Sklootses' to "walk Hinde out." He was working as an apprentice to a shoemaker and the couple had been seeing each other since the spring before. Everyone, it seemed, talked of how they were in love and would be married, but Hinde still blushed violently whenever Jacov appeared at the Sklootses' door.

She would sit on the bed she shared with Rose and twist her fingers together until Zena or Eli would shout, "He's here! It's Jacov! Hin-de! Jacov is here! Weren't you expecting him?"

And Hinde, sure that the whole building had heard, would shyly open the bedroom door and step out into the kitchen with a little nod at Jacov Abramson and at whomever else happened to be in the kitchen at the time.

Then Zena Skloots would offer Jacov a glass of tea with one of her treasured lumps of sugar to bite on as he drank, and they would all sit at the kitchen table and talk until a proper time had elapsed and Jacov could ask Hinde if she'd care to go for a walk with him.

"Tonight!" Lillian said excitedly when Jacov and Hinde had left, bundled in wool wraps against the cold. "He'll ask her tonight!"

Zena nodded. "Moshe said Jacov spoke to him. If Hinde says yes, we will make the arrangements."

" 'If Hinde says yes'!" Lillian cried. "Oh, Mama, do you think Hinde will say *no*?"

"I think," Zena answered, "that Hinde will answer how she feels."

"She will answer how Papa feels, you mean," Rose laughed.

"Now, Rose, your papa has the best in mind for his daughter. That's what papas are for," Zena said.

Rose covered her smile with her fingers while Lillian chattered on:

"Mr. Olshansky has always approved of Jacov Abramson. Hinde knows that or he would have said something to her right away. Look at the way Hinde has changed since she met Jacov! Hasn't she, Mama? Hasn't she, Rose?"

It was true, Rose thought, as she nodded agreement. Dour-faced Hinde now smiled and laughed and fluttered her eyelashes. Hinde was now nineteen—a woman—and she behaved as if she were a young girl! When she was a young girl, Hinde had behaved as if she were nineteen. Or even older. Rose smiled at her thoughts.

"Oh, you're smiling, Rose Olshansky," Lillian teased. "We all know Hinde is going to be proposed to tonight and we all know she will say yes and we all know there's going to be a wedding!" She clapped her hands excitedly, stopping when she saw quiet Anna's face.

"Oh, Anna, you'll be next," Lillian said. "You and Meyer will be next . . ."

Anna kept her eyes lowered. "Meyer has to save more money before we can get married, Lillian. You know that. Lister's place will always be too crowded for us and I cannot live in his wagon with him."

"Oh, but Meyer loves you so!" Lillian sighed dreamily.

"Love, yes, but love doesn't share a room with a horse!" Anna snapped. Then she added softly, " . . . No matter how much you like to dream, little sister. There has to be more than love."

Eli began to rock in his chair and they all turned to look at him.

"A daughter, I'm losing a daughter," he intoned.

Rose winked at Lillian. Whenever he thinks he's losing us, we're daughters, she thought. But it warmed her all the same, just as it had the night she'd been so ill.

"You shouldn't worry, Eli," Zena said, pouring the rest of the tea into his glass and Seltzer into her own. "Some cousin from the boat will fill Hinde's place before her bag is even packed!"

A Truly New Dress ⌒

"You look so pretty, Celia," Fanny said for the fourth time that afternoon. "I never saw a dress as pretty as that! Rose is wonderful!" She began to do a little jig in the middle of the Sklootses' kitchen.

Rose, with a mouthful of pins, nodded her thanks to Fanny. Celia was standing on a chair above them while Rose worked at the hem of the dress she was making for her.

"She'll be the prettiest girl at the wedding!" Fanny cried, genuinely happy for Celia.

"No, I won't," Celia said. "Hinde will be the prettiest girl." But she patted the material lovingly and smiled at Rose.

The dress was made of stiff pink cotton with large puffy sleeves, and there was an enormous matching pink hair ribbon for Celia to pin at the back of her head to hold up her curls.

The door burst open and Mume stepped into the flat. Mume never knocked on any door.

"Well, are you ready?" Mume said. "There's work to be done at home—" She stopped talking and her mouth hung open at the sight of Celia in her pink wedding dress.

"What's this!" Mume cried.

"Mama, this is the dress Rose is making for Celia. For Hinde's wedding!" Fanny said. "You knew Rose was fitting it on Celia today. That's why we're here!"

Mume propped a hand on her hip. "But such a dress!" she snapped. "What does she need something fancy like that for! One month, she'll outgrow it! Waste of good money! Pah!"

Rose, still on her knees, took the last pin from between her lips and carefully slid it into the hem. "I got the fabric from Eli. It was a present," she said softly. "And this is her sister's wedding. She should have something special to wear for her sister's wedding."

"Pah!" Mume said again.

"Oh, Mama, be happy for Celia," Fanny said tenderly. "She looks just like a real princess."

And Celia did look fine in her beautiful dress and in the worn but hole-free shoes that Rose had managed to find for her.

The three young girls all smiled at Mume, who decided to argue no more.

"It's time for them to go home," Mume said to the air above their heads. "I said I was coming for them at five o'clock and it's five o'clock so here I am. So, Rose, if you're finished now?"

"None of This Is Forever" ⟿

Meyer, dressed in the black suit he had bought for the occasion, stood rocking on his heels at the back of the hall on Clinton Street where the Neschvizer met every Sunday night.

A wedding, he thought. The wedding of my sister. He smiled, thinking: This one I am really invited to! He looked down at Rose, standing by his side.

"Remember Papa's wedding, Rosele?" he asked, tilting her chin with his fingers.

"The night we got off the boat," she answered. "Who could forget?" She grinned up at her handsome brother, almost eighteen now and taller than Hinde.

"I got my own place to live that night. The back of a wagon."

Rose nodded. She knew the makeshift stable where Lister's wagon and the horse, Molly, were housed at night. She'd often stopped by to see Meyer on her way to night school—just to visit or to bring him a piece of Zena's cake she'd saved from her own supper.

"Oh, it's not so bad," Meyer said, as if reading her thoughts. "Yes, now I'm taller it's more cramped. Now I have to take everything out of the wagon at night—including shelves—to make room for my legs. But . . . it's quiet. It's a nice quiet, Rosele. Molly will snort or chew some hay or stamp her foot . . . Mostly that's the only sounds I hear. The smells are horse smells, stable smells . . . country smells. It reminds me of home a little. I can fall asleep thinking of mountains and green grass."

Rose nodded, understanding. Very little reminded her of home. "But you are cold in weather like this. I know it," she said.

"Lister's wife, she keeps giving me blankets, quilts—more than I need. She keeps saying she thought I'd be able to be inside by now and she feels bad. I don't mind it so much, Rosele, except when I think that I may be there forever. Then I mind it."

Rose clutched at his wrist. "Meyer, it won't be forever. None of this is forever. I just know it."

"From your mouth to God's ear," Meyer said and patted her shoulder.

A Princess and a Pigeon ⌒

Yette sat with the Resnik family, keeping her arm firmly through Mrs. Resnik's and watching her carefully. The frail woman had insisted on coming to witness Hinde's marriage, and Meyer had brought around Lister's horse and wagon to drive her. It had been a bumpy ride, but Mrs. Resnik had not complained. Yette and Mr. Resnik had walked with the children, including the baby who now slept against Rebecca Resnik's shoulder. Mikey Resnik leaned over and whispered something into Yette's ear. She couldn't understand a word, but she gathered it was one of the silly jokes Mikey was always picking up at school, because he began to giggle through his words. Yette smiled at him.

"That's a good one, isn't it? Isn't it, Yette? Can I tell it to the bride and groom?" Mikey asked.

"Not now, Mikey. Maybe later."

Yette craned her neck for a glimpse of her own family. She hadn't seen any of them for nearly two weeks. There was Rose with Meyer, but where was Baby Celia? Where were Mume and Fanny? Ahh . . . There they were, near the door by which Hinde would enter the hall.

"Ahhh," Yette breathed. There was Celia! Rose had told her Celia would look like a storybook princess and she surely did!

Moshe, her father, stood at the front of the room, his back straight, his red beard gleaming. Another proud occasion for him in full view of his family and friends. In America! In an American building! He was almost puffed with pride, like the silly pigeons Yette was always nearly stepping on in the street.

Different Dreams ⬎

Rose sat at the piano and played, joining the fiddlers for the dancing. Hinde and Jacov began it—solemnly at first, then joyfully, as Jacov swirled Hinde, faster and faster, holding her tightly at the waist. The men did the traditional circle dance to much clapping and applause and, finally, everyone joined in, including the very youngest children, who rode on the feet of their older relatives. Rose laughed and cheered as loudly as anyone as Hinde and Jacov were lifted on chairs high above the crowd and everyone drank toasts to their lifelong happiness.

Anna watched dreamily, longing for the day she and Meyer would be lifted on two chairs. She squeezed Meyer's hand.

Soon everyone was changing partners. Rose left the music to the fiddlers and found herself dancing with the joyful bridegroom.

"Congratulations, Jacov," Rose cried, "and long life!"

"I want it to be a good one, Rose," Jacov said over the music. "—A better one for Hinde and our children than we've known. There are opportunities here, Rose."

Rose stopped dancing. She knew there were opportunities in this new country, but many of them were too vague to her. She wanted an opportunity she could touch! She had mastered *The Prince and the Pauper* and had begun *Oliver Twist*, which she enjoyed more. She knew the feelings of the little boys in the workhouse. Mr. Pratt encouraged her. And he was teaching her mathematics, for which she found she had an aptitude. Learning to read and write and do numbers was a beginning, but a beginning of what?

"Jacov," she said, searching his face, "what do you mean? What opportunities?"

"Ah, Rose, it's a wedding! I have a day off from serious thinking. Let's finish the dance. We can talk one night when we play at Skloots's: I have been officially invited to the weekly card game!"

"Officially!" Rose laughed. Jacov had been attending the men's card game regularly for a long time.

"Moshe made an 'official' invitation!" Jacov was laughing, too. "I think he wanted me to offer to pay dues!"

"Oh, don't you let him get away with that," Rose giggled. "He will if he can, you know."

"Oh, I know your papa, Rose. And what's more, I like him."

Rose grew serious again. She forgot about her papa.

"Tell me, Jacov," she said. "I want to know. How will things be better for Hinde and the children you will have? Will your children be able to go to school and learn things? Not just how to read and write, but great literature and music and—"

"Wait . . ." Jacov smiled down at her. "Great literature—I don't know. But what I would like to see is being able to own my own business and be my own boss . . . Being able to try my own ideas—because they're good ones, Rose. I'm good with my hands, I'm good with the leather. I could make shoes rich men would cry for. And I have ideas about how to sell them, too! Someday, when I have my own shop—you'll see!"

Rose listened as she finished the dance with her new brother-in-law. Everyone's dream was different. Jacov's was to be his own boss, have his own store. That was a good dream . . . to do something on your own, support your family on your own. And if Jacov hired people to help him, he would be kind to them, Jacov would. Not like Mr. Griffin and Mr. Warren and all the managers and contractors of other factories . . .

Rose thought of Isadore Mestrovich and his union talk. Unions would force the bosses to be kind whether they wanted to or not, or they would lose all their workers . . .

Lillian's dreams were of love and marriage, but as Anna and Meyer had both said, life went on after love-and-marriage so your dreams couldn't stop there.

She watched Jacov and Hinde swirl around the room together. She moved toward the table of food and picked up a piece of herring and a chunk of pumpernickel, which she bit into absently. Hinde and Jacov: married now. Jacov had a dream, but meanwhile they would live in a flat much like the flat the Sklootses, the Resniks, her papa and Mume and just about everyone she knew, lived in now: dark and airless, smelly and overcrowded.

Rose thought of Neschviz, which had never offered an easy life. The village was poor and it had been terrifying never to know when a pogrom was on its way. Rose remembered hiding under the hay, hiding in the hills, hiding under beds—sobbing wildly as a toddler, not understanding, while the Czar's soldiers terrorized her family, her neighbors. There were terrible times in the *shtetl*. But it smelled good in summer . . . and everyone knew where he belonged because it was so small . . . little Neschviz. Rose shivered. Gone now. Wiped off the earth, Jacov had said. And all its people were here—and no one felt he belonged . . .

New York City, America. Rose chewed her hard bread. It seemed to her that the differences between the little *shtetl* and New York were that here, the chances were much fewer that she'd be killed. And that here, there was very little that was fresh and green and much that was cold, stone and gray.

Opportunities, Jacov had said. Yes, Rose thought, it stood to reason that there were many more here than in the old country. America was not just New York City, and America was a changing place. The only things that changed in Neschviz were the seasons.

"L'Chaim!" someone next to Rose shouted, raising his glass to the new bride and groom, and Rose jumped, startled out of her thoughts.

"L'Chaim!" she, too, called. "Long life, Hinde and Jacov!" Long life to all of us, she thought, with just a little time in it to sit and think!

Mr. Pratt ⌒

Mr. Pratt nodded at Rose's raised hand.

"I think," Rose said, "that the English of the street is hard enough to master. The English of Mr. Shakespeare is impossible!"

Mr. Pratt threw back his head and laughed. "You of all people should never use the word *impossible*, Miss Olshansky. Look at all you have accomplished in a year! I promise—you will enjoy Mr. Shakespeare, Miss Olshansky."

Mr. Blitzer raised his hand, but spoke before he was recognized.

"I agree with Miss Olshansky," he said. "I don't see the point of reading this Mr. Shakespeare. I would rather learn about—"

"I didn't say I didn't see the point, Mr. Blitzer," Rose interrupted. "I only said—"

"I want to learn more mathematics!" Mr. Blitzer

thundered. "I want to become good enough to keep books! I want—"

"I want that, too, Mr. Blitzer!" Rose shouted. "It's *all* important, don't you see?"

Mr. Pratt tapped his pointer on the desk. "While you two argue, you are wasting our time together. Mr. Shakespeare's language is beautiful and we can learn many things from him. And mathematics is beautiful and helps us every day. Miss Olshansky is right. It is all important. But there is fun, too. I would like this class to read scenes from Shakespeare's plays. To act them out together. To hear language at its best and to have fun!"

Mr. Blitzer sighed. "In our world here, Mr. Pratt, there is no room for 'fun,'" he said. "We need to learn to make our way."

Mr. Pratt made a clicking noise with his tongue. "Very well," he said. "I do understand. I wish—"

"I wish, too, Mr. Pratt," Mr. Blitzer said.

"Well." The teacher put his arms behind his back. "I will see you all day after tomorrow, then."

The students rose from behind the little desks and gathered their books, as they pulled on light coats and shawls.

"Miss Olshansky?" Mr. Pratt called.

Rose looked up.

"Would you like to take home a copy of *Romeo and Juliet?*"

"I would love to, Mr. Pratt. But not tonight. All the men are playing cards at my house and I don't want my papa to catch me with books. I'll have to hide the ones I have as it is."

"Your papa doesn't want you to attend school?"

"Not as long as I'm not paid to attend, Mr. Pratt. May I take the book next time?"

"Of course. Would you like me to hold those for you until our next class?"

Rose clutched them tighter. "Oh, no! Thank you—but no, because then I'd be without them for two whole days."

Between a Father and His Children

Rose heard the growls and the laughter as she mounted the tenement stairs. The growls are losing and the laughter is winning, she thought as she opened the door.

There were the men at the kitchen table. The weekly game of poker. At least, they tried to play every week. Not every man could make it each time, but Moshe never missed. They enjoyed the game, the company and best of all, the fights that broke out. The men loved to fight and could find any occasion worthy of starting one: politics, religion, the goals of the labor unions, the behavior of relatives, the trends of the times, and, of course, the game itself.

Rose took a quick look around the table: Her papa, her new brother-in-law, Jacov Abramson, Eli Skloots, her brother, Meyer, and the Sklootses' new boarder—a landsman named Morris, who slept on a folding cot near the door in the kitchen.

Meyer looked up from his cards and greeted her. "Rosele!"

"And where were you?" Moshe grunted without looking up.

Rose had hidden her books in the folds of her skirt before entering the room and now she pressed her arm tight against them to keep them from dropping.

"Out," she said, trying to sound as casual as she could. "Walking."

"Out walking? Whenever I'm here for cards you're out! Out walking! Out walking at night! You don't have enough to make you tired during the day? Skloots's girls and Zena are in the bedroom sewing! You should be helping. Eli, you have no control over this child?"

Eli Skloots reddened and shuffled the cards he was holding. "Don't talk, Moshe. Play," he said gruffly. "It's getting late already." They were playing for pennies.

Morris, the boarder, yawned loudly. He had considered his cards and folded his hand. "I'm going to sleep," he said. He stood up and moved toward his cot.

"Sit down," Moshe commanded. "We're not through yet."

Morris shrugged. "I'm through."

"You're through when I say you're through," Moshe barked. He was losing.

"Moshe. Let him sleep," Eli said with a wave of his fingers. "He's still the greenhorn. Not used to it here yet."

Moshe snorted. "It'll be a better game when Resnik is back," he grumbled.

"Ah, Resnik," Eli mumbled.

Mrs. Resnik had died two weeks before, leaving Yette with the management of the household and the part-time work in the store. Mrs. Wolf had had her funeral after all.

"What kind of a man quits in the middle?" Moshe continued. "What kind of man, I ask, leaves when the rest of the players are still playing?"

"Papa, let him be," Meyer said soothingly.

Rose took advantage of the argument to pull open a drawer near the basin and slip her books into it. As she closed the drawer silently, Meyer called her name. She whirled, her back against the drawer.

"You take Morris's place, Rose," Meyer said with a grin. "Let Rose play, Papa."

"Don't be foolish," Moshe grunted.

"She's good at numbers," Meyer said. Rose coughed loudly.

"What?" Moshe asked.

"I said, Rose can learn fast," Meyer answered quickly. "Of course, if you're afraid you'll lose to a girl . . ."

Rose opened her mouth to protest and stopped herself. She caught her tongue between her teeth and waited.

Good-natured Jacov beckoned her. "I must stop soon, too, Rose," he said. "Your sister is waiting for me. But your papa would like a chance to get some of his money back, so why don't you sit with us? After this hand."

"This hand is over!" Moshe shouted, throwing his cards down and smashing his fist on the table.

Meyer calmly swept up the pennies in the middle

of the table. "This is my night," he said, "and it's about time."

"Your night? Your night?" Moshe bellowed. "Not yet it's not! Rose! Sit!"

Rose sat quickly in the chair Morris had vacated. "Yes, Papa," she said.

"Listen to me: You will learn this very quickly so we can get on, do you understand? Everyone is tired, so hurry with the learning. Where is your money?"

He did not ask if she had any, only where it was. In fact, she had ten cents, which she kept in a handkerchief, tucked into the top of her shoe. It had taken her a while to accumulate, dividing her money between Eli and Moshe. Eli sometimes let her keep a few cents for herself and sometimes she held back a penny or two if there was a treat she wanted to buy for Celia. She undid her shoe and took out four pennies, counting them carefully. Moshe would be angry if he knew she'd kept as many as ten!

"Good," her papa said. "All right, teach her, Meyer, while I eat something. Don't yawn in my face, Eli, we are not finished yet!"

"Rosele, you know any cards?" Meyer whispered.

Rose shrugged. "I know what the deck looks like, anyway. And how it goes. Ace, king, queen, jack, ten . . ."

"Yes, all right, that's fine. Now here's the way you play this game. You first put down your money, you see? And then there is money in the pot. Then the dealer gives you five cards. You may throw back what you don't want."

93

"How do I know what I don't want?"

"Ah," Meyer said, and explained the kinds of hands it took to win at 5-card draw poker.

Rose frowned, nibbled at her lower lip and listened. "A royal flush," she repeated. "That's down from the top, like I said. Ace, king, queen, jack, ten, right?"

"Right."

"Then . . . a full house?"

"No, no. First a straight flush, then four of a kind, *then* a full house."

"She'll never get all this now, Moshe," Eli complained. "Teach her another time. When it's earlier."

"Now!" Moshe yelled, banging his fist on the table again. "Are you learning this, Rose? Everyone is *tired!*"

"Yes, yes, Papa, I'm learning." She wished she could take out pencil and paper and write down the order of winnings but she couldn't answer to her papa about where she'd learned to write. So she listened to Meyer repeat the order twice more with her eyes squeezed shut in concentration.

Finally she said, "I'm ready," and Eli Skloots blew out his breath in a weary sigh.

"She's ready!" Moshe yelled. "Ante up!"

"Put in two cents, Rosele," Meyer whispered. "That's what we start with."

Rose obediently put two pennies down in the middle of the table.

"Deal, Meyer!" Moshe bellowed. "Come on, come on!"

"All right, Papa, all right . . ."

Meyer dealt five cards to each player, and watched

their faces. Jacov's registered nothing except fatigue. He yawned, discarded and said, "Give me two, Meyer."

Moshe could never hide what he was feeling. It must be a good hand, Meyer thought. I can see the corners of his mouth begin to turn up. In spite of himself, Meyer smiled at his father.

"Nothing for me!" Moshe said in a firm voice and knocked his five cards on the table for emphasis. "I stay the way I am!"

Meyer nodded, trying not to smile. He looked at Eli.

"Oy," Eli said, shaking his head. "I'm out. I'm folding. Nothing but rotten hands all night! I'm keeping my money." He put his cards face down on the table, put his hands behind his head and leaned back in his chair.

"Rosele?" Meyer inquired softly.

"Um," Rose said.

"*Well?*" her father roared.

"Sh, Moshe, you'll wake the building," Eli said, but to no avail.

"*Speak, daughter!*" Moshe insisted.

Rose looked at her hand. Though she had never played poker before, it didn't take experience to know that the three aces she was holding could make her a winner. But she hesitated over her choice. If she *could* beat her father . . . *should* she?

"*R-R-R-Rrrrose!*" Moshe trilled and Rose made up her mind. She discarded her seven of hearts and her six of diamonds. "I'd like two, Meyer, please," she said.

Meyer nodded, smiled and dealt her two cards.

Rose picked them up. The ace of diamonds—the last ace—and the eight of hearts.

Four aces. In the first hand. She looked at her father, who seemed to be chuckling to himself over his cards. Oh, she thought—he could have better. He didn't discard anything. He could still win. A straight flush is better than four of a kind . . . She held her cards tightly and waited.

Meyer looked at his own hand. He discarded and picked up two cards. But he didn't smile at his draw. Not yet. Besides, his father hadn't discarded *any* cards!

"Bet!" Moshe yelled, and Eli, dozing with his chin on his chest, jumped.

"I'm in," Jacov said, and put down two more pennies.

"I'm in! Two cents!" Moshe slammed it down. "Rose!"

"Um," Rose said, looking at her four aces.

" 'Um', she says! 'Um'! No more 'um'! *Bet, daughter!*" Moshe slammed his fist on the table and Eli Skloots jumped again. "Bet or fold! We haven't got time for this maybe, maybe-not!"

Rose took a deep breath. She reached down and tugged at the little handkerchief in the top of her shoe. She hoped with all her heart that her papa would be so absorbed in the game he wouldn't notice her extra money.

As Moshe began to trill her name again with his dramatic rolling *R*, Rose interrupted him.

"All right," she said. "I'm in for two cents—" She put in the last of the four pennies she had shown, and

then: "And I *raise* you two cents!" Down went two
more pennies from her shoe!

Meyer covered his burst of laughter with the back
of his hand.

Moshe's face purpled. "*What?*" he bellowed.

Rose wasn't sure if he was questioning her wealth
or her bet. But she had been right. He was too wrapped
up in his cards.

"Meyer!" Moshe cried. "You explained this game?
You explained to her? Does she know what she's doing?"

"I know what I'm doing, Papa," Rose said firmly.

Meyer had to tighten his lips to hide his smile from
his father. "Well, then," he said, "here's four cents to
cover that and—I raise you two more!" He put down
six pennies.

Rose looked at him from under her lashes.

Moshe grunted loudly. "You, Jacov!" he cried.

"I'm in," Jacov said.

"*I'm* in!" Moshe shouted, tossing four cents onto the
table. A penny bounced and fell in Rose's lap. Meyer
was so close to laughter he had to bite a knuckle.

"*Daughter!*" Moshe yelled.

"Moshe, will you keep down your voice!" Morris
called from his cot. "You can play without the yelling!"

"Quiet, greenhorn!" Moshe said over his shoulder.
"My daughter is betting or folding!"

"I'm betting," Rose said softly, and put down the
last of her ten cents. "Two cents to cover Meyer's
raise . . . and two more."

"Another raise! What is this!"

"Papa, calm down," Meyer cautioned. "Rose is learning." And he coughed to cover his laugh. "Little sister, I'm covering your raise and raising you two more cents," he said.

"Well, I'm out," Jacov said, folding his cards. "Now it's between a father and his children."

Moshe leaned back in his chair. Then forward. Then back again. "Um," he grunted. Rose resisted the impulse to comment on his "um."

Moshe spread his cards and held them higher, in front of his face. It was the best hand he'd held all night. He had to gamble with it, he had to. He had to beat his daughter, but more important, he had to win. He hadn't won at a night of poker in a long time.

Now, when he finally spoke, he didn't yell.

"Four cents," he said, "to cover your raises, and I, your father, raise you two more."

Rose swallowed. Her ten cents was gone. She looked helplessly at Meyer.

"What's wrong, Rosele? Did you make a mistake? It's all right, *shoene-maydele* . . ."

"No," Rose said, "no mistake. I don't have any more money." She looked down at her lap.

"*What?*" Moshe's roar was back.

By this time, Eli Skloots was wide awake. He held up a hand, palm out.

"How much do you need, Rose?" he asked.

Rose answered quickly. "I need four cents to cover Meyer and Papa's raises and two more cents to raise again."

Meyer could no longer conceal his delight and burst into unrestrained laughter.

Eli, too, was grinning happily. "Here you are," he

said, pulling pennies from his pocket. "Six cents for Rose Olshansky with love from her other papa!"

"What is the joke here?" Moshe growled. "I see no joke here! Your bet, Meyer!"

"All right," Meyer managed, wiping tears from his eyes. "All right. Here's two cents to stay in and two to cover Rose's raise." He put his pennies down.

"Now, my children," Moshe said, his voice tight. "I see your two cents and now I call!"

"What?" Rose asked.

"He's calling you, Rosele," Meyer told her. "He wants to see what you've got."

"Can he do that? See what I've got?"

"Yes. Now we see who wins," Eli said. "Put your cards down, Rose."

Rose showed her four aces.

"*AAAAACH!*" Moshe wailed, causing Morris the boarder to leap upright on his cot.

"Oh, Rose!" Meyer cried, happy for her even though he'd lost. "Good for you! See?" He showed her his cards. "I had a full house. I thought I would win, really I did. What did you have, Papa?"

"Never *mind!*" Moshe shouted, but Eli leaned over and peeked before Moshe could hide his cards.

"A straight! See? A two, three, four, five and six!" Eli reported gleefully. "A straight only! You *both* beat him!"

But Rose, her eyes shining, had forgotten her father and his displeasure. She spread her arms, leaned over the table and scooped all the pennies onto her lap.

"Here, Eli," she said, counting carefully. "Six cents. Thank you for your faith in me! . . . Eleven, twelve . . ."

"It's too late," Moshe muttered, getting up from the table. "We never should have played so late."

" . . . Twenty-five, twenty-six, twenty-seven . . ."

"I'm proud of you, Rosele. You can play with us any time," Meyer said, patting her shoulder.

"Any time," Jacov echoed.

"Who said so?" Moshe grunted. "*I* didn't say so."

"But we all agree," Jacov said. "Don't we, Morris?"

"I agree," Morris sighed. "Now can I get some sleep?"

"Thirty-nine, forty, forty-one, forty-two. Forty-two cents! All mine!" Rose clapped her hands and the money jingled in her lap. "When can we play again? This is a wonderful game!"

Moshe, putting on his coat, whirled around. "What is this, a young girl staying up so late! Look how late in the night it is! Eli, have you no control over this child?"

Rose looked at her brother, smiled slightly and lowered one eyelid in a wink.

FIVE

1897

A Meeting ⟶

Hyman Rogoff, halfway through his eighteenth year, had felt himself to be a man since his thirteenth birthday. And if his wiry brown beard didn't prove it, his carriage did—the way he held his shoulders back, his neck straight, his head erect with his chin jutting out, his body leaning slightly forward as he walked or sat, as if he were in a hurry to get where he was going. It was a posture he had devised for himself in America; it helped him to feel that his boyhood was past. Upon meeting him, people usually thought he was older than he was, which made him smile inwardly. Hyman Rogoff rarely smiled outwardly.

He had been born in Volozhen, a Russian industrial town, where he'd worked in a factory—sewing. He'd studied the Talmud and learned to read Hebrew and Polish by himself, and his father and mother and two younger sisters were sure he'd grow up to be a scholar.

That was before they all died in a pogrom. Hyman

had found them when he came home from the synagogue. Their bodies, burned and stabbed, were among the ruins of the wooden shack they had called home. A torch had been thrown through the window, and the family was caught by the Cossacks on horseback as they tried to flee the blazing room. Except for the youngest daughter. She was on the floor near the charred cooking stove, her arms flung over her head.

Hyman had moved further into the town of Volozhen, losing himself in the crowds, working hard into the evening, sleeping in doorways and stables, until he had earned enough for steerage passage to America. He was just thirteen.

There was no one to meet him at the boat, but he hadn't minded. He felt lucky to have survived the voyage. At Ellis Island, the newly opened immigration center, he and hundreds of others were herded into the massive hall that occupied the entire width of the building. They were pushed into dozens of lines, divided by metal railings, where they filed past doctors, inspectors, interpreters. Confused, exhausted, gaunt, Hyman Rogoff nevertheless felt ready for his new life to begin.

It seemed to continue where the old one left off.

New York City was bigger than Volozhen, but there were still crowds, factories, and only doorways to sleep in. Hyman found work with one of the clothingmakers and met his first friend, Isadore Mestrovich. Isadore let him share his Ludlow Street coal cellar until another landsman from the factory took Hyman into his flat.

Isadore brought Hyman to his first union meeting

and that experience fired the boy with a sense of purpose. Already his factory had several small unions of pieceworkers.

Now, at eighteen, on a warm June night, Hyman Rogoff strode resolutely toward the school where meetings with some of the union leaders were held.

These meetings were lively. Everyone had a glass of beer and there were plates of herring and chunks of pumpernickel. The men knocked their glasses together and cheered and argued. Hyman grumbled to himself as he approached the building. He wished they were more serious and accomplished more.

"Ouch!"

Hyman stepped back, startled. He was staring into the frowning face of a chubby young girl of about fourteen. Her dark, thick brown hair was parted in the middle, wound down over her ears and drawn up again into a bun at the back. Her cheeks were very red. He frowned. She looked familiar to him.

"Do you mind?" she asked in Yiddish. "You're standing on my skirt!"

He was so surprised he moved too quickly, nearly tripping over his own feet.

The girl giggled.

"That was quite a dance," she said, and then looked quizzically at him. "Do I know you?" she asked.

"I—uh—" was all he could manage.

"I do. You work at Griffin, don't you?"

"No. Yes. I mean—I did. I did work at Griffin, but now I work at the Allen Street factory." He waited for her to comment, but she didn't. "I—I make buttonholes," he finished.

She giggled again. Hyman frowned at her over his beard.

"I'm Rose Olshansky," she said and smiled at him.

Hyman thought, What a strange girl! There's nothing at all demure about her. It must be because she's very young.

"Well?" Rose demanded.

"Well, what?"

"I've just told you my name. You're supposed to tell me yours. Isn't that the way it goes?"

Hyman took a deep breath. "It's Hyman. Hyman Rogoff."

"Rogoff?"

"Well . . . five years ago when I got here . . . at the boat . . . It used to be Rogovin. They—"

"I know," Rose interrupted with a wave of her hand. "They always change our names when they don't hear you right or they can't pronounce what you've said. And now it's Rogoff? Right?"

"Yes . . . Did they change your name, too?" he asked.

"No. They nearly did, but my brother, Meyer, he heard the man pronounce it wrong: O'Shansey. Like we were Irish. So Meyer said very loud, like this: *Ole-SHAN-skee!* And he made the man repeat it after him. Twice!" She laughed again, and Hyman shook his head. "Well," Rose went on, "we'd better go in or we'll be late!"

"Late? Are you going to the union meeting?" Hyman asked.

"Union meeting! Aren't you going to a night-school class?"

"Night school?"

Rose clapped her hand to her mouth. "Well!" she said. "Same building but different meetings. Goodbye, Mr. Rogoff. It was nice—um, bumping into you!"

"Wait—"

"Yes?"

"You work at Griffin?" Hyman asked.

"Yes . . ."

"Oh. Well . . . No, I mean—that is, I thought I had seen you before," Hyman stammered. "And that's where it must have been. Griffin. Uh—the Griffin Cap Factory."

Rose grinned widely at him. "I know," she said. "I know it's the Griffin Cap Factory. And, yes, that's where you must have seen me. Because that's where I've seen you. And now I have to go, Mr. Rogoff."

Clutching her books with one hand and pulling at her skirt with the other to keep from tripping over it, Rose hurried up the steps into the building. Hyman found himself staring after her with his mouth open. He had met young girls before . . . He had had two younger sisters. And he worked with women, he always had. But . . . this one . . . No girl had ever spoken to him the way this one did! It wasn't that she was brazen . . . No, it wasn't that . . . But she certainly wasn't shy . . . *What* was her name again?

"Rogoff!" Isadore Mestrovich came up behind Hyman and clapped him on the back, startling him out of his thoughts. "Come! We're late! Why are you standing on the steps with your mouth open?"

Hyman said, "Uh—"

"Never mind," Isadore said as they walked toward the door together. "Concentrate on our business. Tonight we're going to talk about a strike at Kahan's."

"Yes," Hyman said, nodding. "A strike at Kahan's. About their foreman, isn't it." But he was thinking: What was her *name*?

A Walk Home ⌒

At the end of the meeting, Hyman went quickly to the door and out into the hall, turning his head from left to right.

"What are you looking for, Hyman?" Isadore asked. "You haven't been your usual arrogant self tonight. People have been talking." He smiled to show he was joking.

"Do you know what time—" Hyman began. He had been about to ask what time the night-school classes were over, but he was overcome by embarrassment.

"What time what?" Isadore asked. "Listen, Hyman —come with us. We're going to Braun's flat—"

Somewhere down the hall, a door opened. The corridor was filled with chatter as people spilled out of the classroom.

"Thanks, Mestrovich. Maybe another time."

"What?"

Hyman absently patted Isadore's arm as he craned his neck at the women in the group. "Another time, Mestrovich, thank you," he said as he moved away from his friend. He had spotted Rose.

"Miss—uh—" he said, falling into step next to her.

"Oh. Mr. Rogoff."

"Your class is over," Hyman said.

"It is . . ."

"And my meeting is over."

"I see . . ."

They had reached the door and he held it for her. They walked out into the warm night.

"Are you going home now?" Hyman asked.

"Of course."

"I was thinking . . . I was wondering if I might walk with you."

Rose tilted her head at him. "Why?" she asked.

"Why?"

Rose nodded.

"Well! Because—because—"

"Because?"

"Because you work at Griffin. And there's been talk of organizing there. And I thought . . . I thought we might talk about that."

They had begun to walk. Rose looked down at her shoes. "You want to talk to me about the union?"

"Isadore Mestrovich is at Griffin. He's my friend. Have you met him?" Hyman asked.

Rose thought. Yes, she remembered Mestrovich. A day during winter. Greasy brown curly hair and a straggly mustache. Intense eyes. Approaching her about the union and nearly getting fired by Mr. Warren. She hadn't seen him since. Or perhaps she had and hadn't thought about it.

"I've met Mr. Mestrovich," she said.

"We're trying to organize all the garment workers into one big union," Hyman said, talking rapidly. "It's very important that everyone stick together. Do you know what we talked about tonight?"

Rose shook her head.

"We want everyone at Kahan's to strike. The knee-pants makers have a terrible foreman there. He tells the Poles that the Jews don't want to work with them, and he tells the Jews the same about the Poles. He's a troublemaker and he should be fired. But he won't be fired unless there is a strike."

Rose nodded. "Yes, well, do you think you can get them to do it?"

"If you ask me," he answered, "I think there is too much talk and play at these meetings and not enough action. I hope for more action soon. What are you learning in night school?"

The transition from one subject to another was abrupt. Rose thought this young man was abrupt. But she answered calmly, "English. Mathematics. Literature."

"Why?"

Rose made a face at him. "You sound like my sisters and almost everyone I know. I can read and write English. Can you?"

"I can read and write Polish and Hebrew . . ." he answered defensively.

"That's fine, but you *live* in America. Don't you think it would help to learn the language and culture of the country you live in?" They had arrived at the stoop of Rose's tenement and she stopped walking to face him.

"Well, what good is all that going to do you! You're a girl! You're going to get married and have babies and take care of your family, right?"

"Oh!" Rose stamped her foot. "You're even *worse* than my father, because you're younger and you should have more advanced ideas!"

"I *do* have advanced ideas!" he shouted. "Don't you think the union is an advanced idea? Why, by the time our children are working there will be better conditions for *all* labor!"

"*Whose* children?" Rose questioned.

"Mine! Ours! Yours and mine! You know what I mean!" Hyman cried, flustered.

"Well," Rose said more softly, "I don't know about your children, but mine will be well-educated. And fine-spoken. And they will love the arts. And they will have music lessons—"

"Mine will own businesses! They will be good bosses! They will buy land! They will—" He stopped and looked around. "Why are we standing here?" he asked. "It is late. Your family will be worried. I must see you home."

"I *am* home," Rose said, straightening her shoulders. "This is where I live. I'm going inside because you're right, it is late. But I think you're a person very . . . very . . ." She thought a moment before continuing—"very much filled up with yourself. And backward, too! Good luck with your union and thank you for walking me home."

She rushed up the steps and was inside the door before he could say another word. He kicked at the stone step. "What kind of a girl is this!" he said aloud. Finally, after some seconds of teeth-grinding and pounding his fist into his palm, he turned and headed back toward his own flat.

When I see her again, he said to himself, I will tell her—I will tell her—

He stopped short. He couldn't remember her last name—or her first. She had told him. She had. It sounded Irish. It was *O* something, but that was all he remembered.

Well, at least he knew where she worked—and where she lived!

An Empty Room at Lister's ⤳

Rose stormed up the stairs loudly and threw open the Sklootses' door. She slammed it shut.

Eli, Zena and Lillian looked up from the kitchen table where they had been having tea and cake.

"So, Rose. A bad night at school?" Zena asked. "Have a glass of tea and some sugar."

"It will sweeten your mood," Lillian said with a smile as she poured for Rose.

"My mood is fine," Rose growled and flopped into an empty chair. "Is Anna sleeping?"

"Anna is out celebrating! Lister's son and his son's wife and their little girl—they are moving out of Lister's flat!"

Rose sat up. "Since when?"

"Tonight Meyer found out. Lister's son got a new job in a paper box factory and it pays more money and he had some money put aside, so—" Lillian's face had turned red, she was talking so rapidly.

"So," Rose interrupted, "there is one empty room at Lister's, right?"

"That's right! But not for long . . ."

"Ahhh," Rose said. "We'll be real sisters now, won't we, Lillian? Meyer will marry Anna soon?"

"Very soon!" Lillian cried.

"No one has said!" Zena snapped. "Stop telling the news before it happens!"

Lillian pursed her lips and sank into her chair.

"Oh, it will be soon, I'll bet, Zena," Rose said, patting her on the arm.

"Well. You cheered up from your slamming-the-door mood, Miss Olshansky," Eli said. It was one of his rare sentences. He hardly spoke when the women were chattering.

"That's right, Rose!" Lillian cried. "What happened at night school to make you so angry?"

Rose sighed. "It wasn't night school, Lillian. There was a man I met who made me angry."

Lillian sat up straight. "A man? What man?"

"He's very stiff—and he frowns, like this." Rose drew her eyebrows together comically and stuck out her jaw in an imitation of Hyman. "And he makes speeches at me and . . . He made me angry."

"Where did you meet this man, Rose?" Zena asked with maternal concern. "Was he in your class?"

"Oh, no. He doesn't believe in learning for its own sake. And especially for women, who are 'just going to get married and have babies'! No, he was at a union meeting in the same building."

"What was his name?" Lillian asked.

"Rogoff."

Lillian giggled. "Was that his first name?"

"No. Hyman."

"I know him," Lillian said, nodding. "He's a friend of Mestrovich. You are right about how he looks. Very determined."

"Oh, yes. That's Rogoff, all right."

"I've never seen him smile."

"I'm sure he doesn't know how." Rose folded her arms and sat back in her chair. "It wasn't even what he said, it was the way he said it that made me so angry!"

"Well, don't think about him then," Lillian said.

"You're right," Rose said. "Think about happy things, like weddings . . . Anna and Meyer, for example . . ."

"The Stones Are Shaking" ⌁

It was hot, that summer of 1897. Celia and Fanny waved paper bags in front of their faces as they moved slowly among the carts on the street. Mume had given Fanny a sugar bun and a piece of ice to suck on, both of which she was sharing with Celia.

"My hands are sticky," Celia said. "I wish I could wash them . . ."

"Wipe them on your paper sack," Fanny said with a shrug. "I don't care if my hands are sticky—the bun is good!"

"I'll wash them at the Resniks'," Celia said absently. "Yette will probably have ice . . ."

"Look, Celia, the street is melting," Fanny said, pointing. "The stones are shaking in the sun!"

"It looks like that, doesn't it?" Celia said. "But it's only a mirage."

"A what?"

"A 'mirage.' It's a French word. It means 'optical illusion.' Something that looks real but isn't."

Fanny shook her head. "I don't remember learning that," she said.

"Rose told me," Celia said. "She learned it at night school. Rose is getting smarter all the time. I'm trying to keep up with her."

Fanny closed her lips tightly. She didn't want to hurt Celia by voicing her thoughts. She privately agreed with Moshe and Mume and others of the family who would never approve of schooling past a certain age for girls. She and Celia were ten and would probably stop school and go to work full time in another two years.

Fanny looked up. They were nearing the Resniks' building. She and Celia were to spend the afternoon helping Yette, whose work with the Resnik children and the Resnik grocery store seemed never-ending.

That's what Celia's life will be like, Fanny thought. And mine, too. The only difference is, the children will be our own, not someone else's. So why bother with all this school business, anyway? We're all going to end up just like Yette!

Yette ⌣⌐

She had finally gotten the youngest Resnik, Tudrus—little Teddy—to nap. He had fallen out of the bed twice, cried, thrown a cup across the room and pulled Yette's hair out of its bun before collapsing into sleep, soaked in perspiration. The other children were out, playing in the streets. Yette could hear their happy cries—she winced with each one, hoping they wouldn't wake the baby.

There was washing to be done, she needed to make over two shirts, mend socks, help for at least a little while in the store and somehow have supper ready for five hungry children and their father in a few short hours.

Yette covered her mouth with her fingers, startled to find herself close to tears.

I shouldn't think this way, she scolded. I shouldn't be feeling sorry for myself. Everyone works hard, everyone!

"Yette!" she heard from the hall. "Yet-te! We're here! Open the door!"

Yette caught her breath. Celia and Fanny—she'd forgotten they were coming to help today. Quickly she wiped at her eyes and went to the door.

"Shhhhhhh!" she whispered as she opened it. "I finally got Tudrus to sleep." She motioned the girls in with her hand, and they tiptoed toward the kitchen table.

"See that pile of clothes next to the stove?" Yette asked softly. "There are holes in everything."

"Don't worry," Celia whispered back, "we'll fix them. Do you have to go to the store? Go ahead. Fanny and I will watch Teddy."

Yette wanted to say "Thank you," but her eyes had filled again and her voice felt choked. Fanny and Celia, already threading needles, did not notice.

"And Hinde said she's coming tomorrow with a

challah, so maybe that will save you some baking time, Yette . . ." Celia continued.

Yette nodded.

"And Meyer and Anna and Rose will come by on Sunday and take all the children to Neschvizer if you want to stay home and get some rest," Fanny added.

"Rest! I have no time to rest—there's too much to do," Yette blurted. It wasn't what she meant to say. She'd meant to say she was grateful.

"Then you'll have some peace to do it in," Celia said. "Now go, Yette. Go on, go to the store. Everything here will be done. Don't worry."

Yette looked at the two young girls bent over the Resnik children's torn clothes. Then she turned quickly and left the flat.

Fanny's mentioning Anna and Meyer had upset her. They had been married just a few weeks and the glow that Anna radiated pained Yette. She longed to share their happiness, but even more, she wanted that kind of happiness for herself. Meyer was younger than she—she should have been married first!

The hall of her building was stifling. She moved to the top of the stairs and leaned against the wall. She took a deep breath and smelled onions.

I don't want to go to the store, she thought. I don't want to be here. I don't know where I want to be but it isn't here!

Yette gritted her teeth, willed herself to stop her petty thoughts. She swallowed hard. I will go, she thought, nodding resolutely. I will go—

"Yette! Mikey's outside crying! That Rubenstein boy pushed him down and he scraped his forehead on the cobblestones—" A neighbor was climbing slowly up the stairs and leaning heavily on the bannister. "He's all right, but you go have a look, yes?" she asked.

"Yes," Yette said, "I'm on my way to the store, anyway . . ." and then, in spite of her good resolve, thought: I'm only nineteen years old!

Another Meeting ⟋⟍

It was still light when the workers at the Griffin Cap Factory left for the evening. Rose found Lillian and Anna in the crowd and tucked her arms through theirs.

"Let's go home!" she sighed wearily. "Anna, when we get to Lister's, can we come up with you and get something to drink? I'm so thirsty I just might faint!"

"Letty Golub *did* faint," Lillian told them with wide eyes. "She fell right off her stool onto the floor!"

"I would be surprised if she were the only one," Anna said, "in this heat." She fanned herself with her hand as the three began to walk toward their homes.

Suddenly, a young bearded man appeared in front of them and they stopped.

"Hello!" the man said too loudly and only to Rose.

Lillian and Anna released Rose's arms and stepped away, looking at her quizzically.

"Hello, Mr. Rogoff," Rose said calmly. "These are my—sisters Anna Olshansky and Lillian Skloots."

Hyman Rogoff bowed stiffly and mumbled, "Ladies . . ." Then he smiled broadly. "Olshansky!" he said, and snapped his fingers. "That's your name!"

"Yes . . ."

"Ah! But . . . Miss Skloots? Your sister?"

"I live with the Sklootses," Rose answered. "And Anna has recently married my brother, Meyer. Lillian and Anna have always been like sisters to me," she added. She drew the girls close to her again. "It's nice to see you, Mr. Rogoff. Good evening." She tried to step past him, but he blocked the way.

"I was wondering if I might—" He stopped, embarrassed. His face was red above his beard.

"If you might what?"

Hyman wrung his hands together. "—if I might— if we might—well, Miss Olshansky, it's very hot, and I thought maybe I might buy you something cold to drink," he said rapidly.

Now Rose was embarrassed. She glanced from Lillian to Anna but they had averted their smiling faces.

"No, thank you," Rose said. "I must go home and help with supper."

"Oh, that's all right!" Lillian piped. "I'll help Mama!"

Rose kicked at Lillian's ankle from under her skirts. "I really think I should get home," she repeated.

"Oh, go ahead," Anna said with a smile. "You were just complaining about how thirsty you were. I'm sure Mama won't mind, will she, Lillian?"

"But—"

"Now, you heard Anna . . ." Lillian returned the little kick with the toe of her boot.

"All right, Mr. Rogoff." Rose glared fiercely at Lillian and Anna. "I would like that very much."

Hyman held out his arm stiffly. Rose took it and marched him off, leaving the two girls giggling on each other's shoulders behind them.

"He reminds me of one of Celia's little stick-man drawings," Lillian chuckled. "The way he leans forward when he walks. Formal, but funny at the same time!"

"But don't they look sweet together," Anna observed, and they giggled again.

A Glass of Seltzer ⟿

He took her to a tiny kosher restaurant on East Broadway. They sat at a front table for two near the window and Hyman ordered two Seltzers for them, which arrived in thick clear glasses. Neither had spoken a word since they'd left Anna and Lillian.

Finally, Hyman, who had downed half his Seltzer in one gulp, leaned toward Rose. "I must confess to you that I had forgotten your name," he managed.

Rose shrugged. "I gathered," she said and sipped her drink.

"I tried so hard to remember it," Hyman said. "But now I will. It's Olshansky!"

"I know," Rose replied.

Hyman coughed. "But your first name I still can't remember," he mumbled.

"It's Rose." She sighed and shook her head.

"Rose!" he beamed as if she had given him a present.

"Ah!" Rose said, and her eyes twinkled. "You can smile!"

"You think I am so serious?"

"Yes. And arrogant."

"You're angry with me because I said I think your

night school is a waste of time? Learning things which you will not use, when your energies could be better spent changing society? What good is reading Dickens, when you could be organizing your floor of pieceworkers?"

"Yes!" Rose looked him in the eye. "That's why."

Hyman looked confused. "That's why what?" he asked.

Rose laughed. "That's why I think you're arrogant. Learning is never a waste of time, Mr. Rogoff. Thank you for the Seltzer and goodbye." She stood up.

He reached over, grabbed her wrist and pulled her down again. She stared at him with her mouth open.

"I'm sorry! I'm so sorry—" he stammered. "It's just that—I don't—I didn't want you to leave. This is just where we left off last time—"

"And where we will always leave off," Rose added. "Why do you want me to stay?"

"Because—I like you!" he blurted.

Rose opened her mouth again.

"I do! I can't forget about you, Miss Olshansky. Most girls are not like you. May I ask how old you are?"

"Fourteen," Rose answered.

"Well, you seem very—determined for a young girl."

"How old are you?" Rose demanded.

"I'm eighteen. Almost nineteen."

"I don't think determination has anything to do with age. Anyway, you're determined, too. We're determined about different things." Rose finished her drink with a large slurp from her straw.

"I would like," Hyman said slowly, "to start again.

To know more about you. I like—to see you laugh.
You are . . . very pretty when you laugh."

"I'm not pretty at all," Rose said firmly. "Don't flatter me with words like that."

"It's not flattery, it's true!" Hyman snapped. "You are *shoene*. I thought so from the very beginning!" He glared at her.

Rose burst into laughter, which caught him off balance until at last he joined her and they sat, grinning at each other across the small metal table.

"Let me get you another Seltzer," Hyman offered and raised his hand for the waiter.

"Oh, no. No, thank you," Rose said. "Only one. I might get sick if I have more than one glass of Seltzer at a time."

"You can get drunk on Seltzer?" Hyman asked, bewildered.

"No." Rose smiled at him. "But—when I was younger I drank too much and blew up like a great balloon!" She puffed out her cheeks, crossed her eyes and held her arms out in a circle to demonstrate.

Hyman laughed. "Did you really?"

"Yes! All the bubbles collected inside me! I have been careful ever since."

"Oh—" His eyes suddenly softened. "But that must have been painful . . ."

"It was. But now I can laugh about it. Lillian showed me what I looked like later. She still teases me about it. She says she could have bounced me!"

He reached across the table and touched her fingers. "Once," he said, "my hand was swollen. It was twice its size. I couldn't sew for over a week."

120

"Was it a sickness?" Rose asked.

"Oh, no, it was a —" He stopped suddenly and blushed.

"A what?"

"Oh, just a—a kind of bite."

"A bite? A rat? Celia, my little sister, was bitten by a rat shortly after we arrived in New York. We were so frightened, we—"

"It wasn't a rat . . ."

"A dog? Sometimes they carry diseases—"

"Not a dog."

"No? What then?"

"A mosquito."

"A what?"

"A mosquito bite. I am allergic . . . I guess . . ."

Rose didn't know whether to laugh or not. A mosquito bite causing such a reaction! And his poor face was redder than ever. She looked down. His fingers were still touching hers. Ever so lightly, but—were they trembling? Impulsively, she slipped her hand over his and squeezed it a little. They smiled at each other over their empty glasses.

Mume's Brother 〜

Rose was home later than she'd expected to be and she hurried up the stairs. But the Sklootses' door flew open before she could touch the knob.

"Rose!" Zena cried as soon as she saw the startled girl. "I thought I heard you on the stairs. You must go to your papa's house right away!"

Rose gasped. "Something's happened to Papa!" She pressed her fingers to her lips.

"No! No, no," Zena reassured her. "Nothing like that. But he was here. Moshe was here to get you. Right after work. He was angry that you didn't come home with Lillian."

"He didn't tell me he was coming," Rose told her.

"I know, I know, but you know your papa. He comes for you, he expects you to be here. Mume's brother has arrived. From the boat. Mume's brother, Levi Samuelson."

Rose looked blank.

"They didn't tell you he was coming?"

"Why should they tell me?" Rose asked. She was tired and hot. She wanted to come inside, but Zena kept her standing in the hall.

"Well, you have to go there right away. Moshe wants Levi to meet his family. There's a party."

"Aren't you going?" Rose asked. "And Eli and Lillian?"

"This is just for Moshe's children. We'll meet Mr. Samuelson another time. Now, Rose, you must go. Don't make Moshe angrier. You'll have your supper there."

"All right." Rose sighed and turned back toward the stairs. She grumbled to herself as she made her way down. "Mume will give me some tea and a piece of bread. Some supper!"

A neighbor's child appeared in the hall and called, "Hello, Rose!"

"Hello, Hannah," Rose answered absently. "Mume's

brother arrives and we all must run to meet him. But how did Mume greet us when we arrived? Ah, well." She sighed again. "We will be there. We will be there to greet Mume's brother."

"Second-class!" ⌒

"You are late!" Moshe growled through his teeth. "How can you embarrass your father! I was to get you and you were not there! Ahhhh!" His voice suddenly became silky and tender. "This is my Rose, Levi," he said to a balding man of about thirty, with milky blue eyes. "The only one of my children you haven't met. She rushed right over. And here she is. Rose. Say something to Levi, Rose!"

"Hello, Mr. Samuelson," Rose said.

Levi Samuelson nodded his head. He took Rose's hand and kept nodding.

"From Grodna, he came!" Moshe boomed. "But not like us! Oh, no! Levi Samuelson, he came on the boat *second-class!*"

"Oh, yes?" Rose said. But she was already turning her head to greet her brother and sisters who were standing quietly in the small kitchen, sipping tea and smiling at her.

Mume bustled over. "You met Levi, Rose," she said, clutching at her brother's arm. "Handsome, isn't he?" Levi blushed. "This is no ordinary man. This is a man with *prospects*! Levi is a *butcher*! He is already able to get a store of his *own*!"

"That's nice," Rose said. "Oh, Celia!" She bent to hug her little sister, who stuffed a bit of cake into Rose's mouth.

"It's good to see you, Rose," Celia said warmly.

"And you, too! Meyer, Hinde!"

Meyer kissed her cheek. "You're late, Rosele," he whispered in her ear. "A mortal sin!"

Rose squeezed his waist. "Where is Yette? Oh—over there in the corner! Yette, are you hiding?" She moved toward her older sister, but Moshe grabbed her arm.

"Levi is staying with us for a while," he said, "but not for long. We think he can get the store on Cherry Street. Rumbaugh's place. And he can live in the back. *Of his own place*, Rose. His *own store!*"

"That's nice," Rose said again. "Yette?"

Yette came shyly to Rose's side, but she was watching Levi, whose hands were clasped tightly together. He looked abashed to be the center of such attention.

"It's nice for Mr. Samuelson, isn't it?" Yette said to Rose with a little smile. "Just arrived and a business of his own already?" She swallowed. "A smart man. Isn't he?"

"*Very* smart," Mume said, but only to Rose.

"Where is Jacov, Hinde?" Rose called to her sister.

"Never mind Jacov!" Moshe hissed in Rose's ear. "You're not here to see Jacov!"

"He's working tonight," Hinde answered. "It was very busy at the shop today. He has some shoes that must be ready by tomorrow."

"Here, Rose, have some tea," Fanny said, slipping

between Rose and her father. "You probably haven't had any supper yet, have you?"

"Thank you, Fanny," Rose said, taking the glass from the little girl. "I'm all right."

"Rose is all right. She's fine, isn't she Levi? A fine girl," Moshe said.

"I think . . ." Yette said haltingly, "that it is . . . very fine to come all prepared to a new country . . ." She looked at Levi and then at her father. "Don't you think? Papa?"

"I think it is fine that Resnik let you come tonight, Yette. Minding the children all by himself so you could come to your family."

Yette turned scarlet. "I mind them all day," she said, looking at the floor. "And he has Becky to help."

"Levi!" Moshe cried. "You should see Rose's handiwork! The things she can sew! Eli says what an asset she is to his business!"

Levi nodded and smiled.

Yette stared at him.

Rose rolled her eyes.

"Quiet Men Are Very Deep" ⟞

"Tell me, Rose," Lillian begged as she bounced excitedly on her bed. "What was he like? Mume's brother?"

Rose laughed. "I don't know," she said.

"What do you mean, you don't know? You went over there—you met him—didn't you?"

"I met him, yes, but I never heard him speak a

word. I never knew anyone so shy, Lillian! Of course, Papa did all the talking, anyway . . . And I guess he must be rich because he came over second-class and has the money to buy his own store . . ."

"His own store? Oh, Rose! What does he do?"

"He's a butcher."

"How wonderful! Always there will be meat on the table! He didn't speak a word?"

"Not a word."

"Poor man! But I'm sure he's exhausted from his voyage. And to have to meet all those strangers—they are, even if they're family, right? And your papa can be so—so—"

"I know how Papa can be," Rose said.

"Well, I'm sure Mr. Samuelson must be a wonderful man," Lillian finished.

"Why are you sure of that?" Rose laughed.

"Well . . . he just sounds . . ."

"*What*, Lillian?" Rose persisted. "You haven't even met him yet!"

"Quiet men are very deep," Lillian said firmly.

"Oh, really?"

Lillian nodded. "And tender. And kind. And understanding. And—"

But Rose was laughing so hard Lillian stopped.

"Lillian Skloots!" Rose cried as she threw a pillow at her. "It's very late! Please go to *sleep* to do your dreaming!"

"Oh, Rose—" Lillian threw the pillow back. "You have no romance in your head!"

SIX

1898

Celebrations ⟿

Lillian and Rose sat on their beds and worked together
on a quilt for Eli.

"I'm glad the quilt is so big," Lillian said. "We can
work with it spread over our laps and warm ourselves
at the same time."

"It *is* cold," Rose said and shivered a little. "I hope
Hinde doesn't get sick in this weather. This is the
coldest winter I can remember."

"Hinde!" Lillian laughed. "Hinde keeps fanning herself with her shawl! She says her body temperature
has gone way up with all the weight she's gained!"

Hinde and Jacov were expecting a baby in April,
and piled next to the dry goods for Eli were all the
baby things Rose and Lillian had made for the coming
event.

"A new baby," Lillian sighed. "I just can't wait until
we're actually aunts, Rose! All this happiness for our
families—I still can't believe it." She bit off the end
of her thread.

"Yette isn't very happy," Rose said.

"Mama says Mr. Resnik wants to marry her . . . He's a nice man. He has his own grocery store . . . and his children are sweet . . . She's been there so long, Rose . . ."

"I know. But I think Yette wants something else."

"What else?"

"I think Yette wants Levi Samuelson," Rose said.

"Levi Samuelson? But Mume and your papa want him for *you*!" Lillian said with a smile.

"Oh, stop!"

"You know it's true! Your papa brings him here for the card games and he's always trying to push you together!"

"I can't imagine why," Rose sighed. "It embarrasses both of us so much. Of course, I can only tell Mr. Samuelson is embarrassed because he turns red. I still haven't heard him say anything."

"Oh, he does . . ." Lillian said.

"Really? What?"

" 'I'm in.' 'I fold.' 'I raise.' "

They both laughed.

"But he's nice," Lillian said. "He has a very nice smile. And when I bring him something to eat or drink he always says 'thank you' so politely. I believe he has lovely thoughts inside his head. I always thought so from the first time you described him."

"Well, I haven't time to read his mind."

"Oh, I know." Lillian pushed her needle in and out of the quilt. "You're too busy with work . . . and school . . . and Hyman Rogoff . . ."

"Sh!" Rose said. "No one knows about Hyman Rogoff, Lillian, and don't you tell!"

Hyman had never come to the Sklootses' flat, but most evenings after work and after every night-school class, Rose found him waiting for her on the sidewalk, leaning against a wall or a post, and snapping to attention as soon as he caught sight of her.

"I don't care for him that way," Rose told Lillian. "We argue all the time."

"Well, why do you see him, then?" Lillian asked.

"I don't. He sees me. He's always there, that's all."

"You could walk away if you wanted to," Lillian teased. "But you don't . . ."

"He's an interesting person. I don't agree with his views at all, but he presents them very well. I learn things from him."

"Oh. He's a teacher, then."

"Yes. A teacher."

"And that's all."

"That's *all*!"

"Classes every evening?"

"Now, don't you start your dreaming over me, Lillian," Rose warned.

"Well, I think you're in love, that's what I think, Rose Olshansky!"

Rose put down her work. "You want everyone to be in love," she said, "and not everyone is!"

Lillian's smile faded. She caught her lower lip between her teeth and bent to her sewing. Rose reached across and touched her hand.

"Oh, Lillian," she said with affection, "you lovely

dreamer. I'm not angry with you. I love you just the way you are. Don't change. I don't mind how you tease me. I want all your dreams to come true. Everyone will fall in love and flowers will bloom in our paths as we walk down the road of life! All right?"

"That sounds fine to me," Lillian answered seriously.

A Marriage Proposal ⟶

Mume Olshansky sat at the Resnik kitchen table and tapped her fingers impatiently on its surface as she watched Yette, across from her, crying softly into a large rag.

"I don't understand you, Yette," Mume sighed. "You should be a happy girl."

But Yette only cried harder and shook her head.

"A nice man, Resnik is. Hard-working. Already established with his own business. A big place here—" Mume waved her arm around the room. "What more could anyone want! Count your blessings, sit up and put your handkerchief away."

Yette bent over the table and buried her face in her arm.

"Weeks and weeks ago he spoke to your papa!" Mume said. "He's not going to wait forever! Yette—you have to get married sometime! Why not to Resnik? Then all these children you have been raising, they'll be yours! Look at *me*! Didn't I take on all your father's children when I married him?"

Inside the crook of her arm, Yette smiled wryly to herself.

"A woman marries a widower," Mume went on unheeding, "that's what happens. She takes on his family."

"But I don't want to marry a widower," Yette said, lifting her face to meet Mume's eyes.

"So? What do you want?"

Yette drew in her breath. "Why couldn't I marry Levi? Why couldn't I marry Levi Samuelson?" she blurted.

Mume's jaw dropped. "My brother? *My brother*? You?"

"Yes, me! What's wrong with me? I'm the second oldest daughter, not Rose! Why are you pushing Levi to marry Rose? I can see it. You don't fool me! Why not me? I'm next! I'm next, Mume—"

"Stop it!" Mume interrupted. "Stop it now, Yette. Levi is not for you."

"But why?" Tears filled Yette's eyes again.

Mume exhaled loudly through her nose and regarded the girl before her. She frowned. Yette was right—she was the second daughter, unmarried and next in line. But Mume had never even considered Yette for her beloved brother, Levi. Yette had a flat and a man. All that was needed was for the ceremony to take place. And besides, Yette was . . . Yette was . . .

"Why are you looking at me like that?" Yette asked. "You haven't answered my question, Mume. Why not me?"

Why not you? Mume thought to herself. Because you remind me of the bees we used to keep when I was a little girl back in the *shtetl*. You are like the dull worker bee. The drone. Necessary but not special. Rose—Rose is like the queen. Rose is special. A mind of her own she has. Rose would be an asset for my Levi, someone to stand at his side, someone to think with, to talk to. A pain in my neck, she is, but for Levi, a good wife. For Levi, the best. But she couldn't say that to Yette.

To Yette she said: "So tell me what's wrong with Resnik."

"He's old! And he has no front teeth! He's like a father to me, it's like I'm his oldest child. He only asked me to marry him because I'm here, because I've always been here, because the children know me, because it's easier! That's the only reason. He doesn't care anything about me!"

"Oh, Yette, don't be such a baby," Mume snapped. "Caring, shmaring! You have to make a life for yourself as Hinde has done. You have already someone to take care of you! You won't even have to move anything!" Mume watched Yette's shoulders heave with sobs and she softened her tone. "Yette," she said, "Levi is not for you. He's a stranger to you; Resnik is a friend. Be practical. This is your home. A man and a business you've already got. Everyone should have it so good. Shrug your shoulders, Yette," Mume sighed, "and get on with your life."

"I Put My Cards on the Table" ⌐

One evening in February, Rose stood on the stoop of the Sklootses' building, facing Hyman angrily. Her teeth were chattering and she wasn't sure if it was from the biting cold of the city streets or from her outrage.

"But you were a scholar!" she cried. "I don't see how you could give up your love of books"—she snapped her fingers—"just like that."

"You're being ridiculous!" Hyman replied. "Do you remember those old men of the village? Sitting around the shul all the time, praying, reading, spending days, weeks, months, arguing as if their lives depended on it—over one small passage in the Holy Book? Do you remember, Rose Olshansky? What did it get them? Is that a way to spend one's life? And does it matter, the interpretation of that passage? Scholarly things have no place in the real world!"

"No place for scholars? No place for art and music, for jokes and games? No place for books? Oh, you stupid man, would you have us all walk around the way you do—like dried-up prunes? Doing nothing but wailing about the state of our lives—?"

"I'm doing more than just wailing! The unions are growing stronger every day. And myself, I've got a pushcart now. I'm working even harder, earning more money—"

"That's all very well. But life isn't only business and causes. We don't only have brains and stomachs! We also have hearts! The heart needs nourishment, too!"

He opened his mouth to answer her, then closed it again.

She glowered at him.

"I guess—you'd better go in . . . You look so cold . . ." he said.

"I guess I'd better."

"Good night, Rose Olshansky."

"Good night, Hyman Rogoff."

Rose turned, wrapping her shawl tighter around her, and went into the building. She skipped up the stairs. They always had the same argument, but she liked Hyman more and more.

When she opened the Sklootses' door, she found the usual group of men around the kitchen table playing cards.

"Hello," she sang at them.

"Again, late," Moshe muttered, and looked across the table at Levi Samuelson, who was studying his cards.

"Come join us, Rose," Meyer offered. "Sit down."

"Thank you, Meyer, not tonight. I'm—"

But Moshe interrupted her. "The game is over now," he announced, folding his hand. "Sit, daughter."

Eli Skloots threw his arms in the air in a great shrug. "The game is over because Moshe Olshansky has a losing hand!" he moaned. "What kind of a way is that to play cards with your friends, Moshe, I ask you!"

"I did not have a losing hand," Moshe lied. "The game is over because Rose is here and I have been waiting for my daughter."

"Waiting for me, Papa?"

"And so has Levi. He says he never sees enough of Rose, isn't that what you said, Levi?"

Levi opened his mouth and closed it again.

"Hello, Levi," Rose said cheerfully.

"He says how can he think of marriage with someone he never sees enough of!" Moshe bellowed.

"Papa!" Rose gasped.

"Papa!" Meyer cried.

Levi's mouth opened and stayed that way.

"Well, why beat the bush around?" Moshe said, waving his arm. "I put my cards on the table! Hah!" He slapped his five cards on the table and barked at his own pun. "Marriage is what we want, we might as well say so! I say so! What do *you* say?"

But Rose didn't say anything. She squinted her eyes in anger and humiliation and tightened her lips.

"Papa, this is not the time or the place to—" Meyer began, but Moshe wouldn't let him finish.

"So where is the time or the place? Rose is always 'out'! Out! Levi comes to see her, what does he see? A bunch of old men playing cards! A butcher, he is, with his own place! A man ready for marriage!"

"Moshe," Eli said, "such yelling. You'll wake Zena and Lillian."

"Zena and Lillian are in the other room sewing, where good women should be! Where Rose would be if—she—got—married!"

"That's enough, Papa," Meyer said. "Look at Rose and Levi—look at their faces, how you make them feel."

"I said what I had to say. What a papa has to say. You heard, Rose?"

"I heard!"

"Don't talk back to your papa! Did you hear?"

"I heard!"

"I said don't talk back! Did you hear?"

Rose nodded.

"Good. Now we leave." Moshe pulled Levi Samuelson out of his chair by his sleeve. The two men wrapped themselves in their large coats and left the flat. Moshe didn't look back. Levi gave the room a pained smile before closing the door.

Eli raised his arms again. "The game is over, just like that." He peered at the cards Moshe had spread on the table. "I was right. He had a losing hand. I was winning!"

"He had to do his matchmaking, Eli," Meyer laughed. "I'm sorry, Rose . . ."

Rose sank into one of the vacant chairs and Meyer put an arm around her shoulders.

"It's Mume's idea, you know," he said with a grin.

"But Mume hates me," Rose said. "Why has she picked *me* for her rich and successful brother?"

"Mume doesn't hate you, Rosele. She only felt that way when she thought we were going to take the food out of her Fanny's mouth. She really admires you."

"Mume doesn't admire anyone!" Jacov laughed.

"Oh, I know you'd never know it. Mume's compliments are reserved for Fannele. But a dummy she isn't. She knows Rose would be a good wife for any man, especially one on his way up like Levi! What do you think of him, Rosele?"

Rose's laugh was a little bark. "He's never said a word, Meyer! Not even 'How do you do?'! How could I think anything?"

"You'll like him, Rose," Morris put in. "He hardly speaks when we play cards, too. A man who doesn't talk—marry him, Rose."

Rose made a face at Morris.

"Well, you're next, Rosele," Meyer said. "Hinde, me, soon Yette—Mume and Papa want everyone taken care of!"

Rose's eyes blazed. "Meyer, I don't want to get married," she said.

"What are you saying, Rose?" Eli said. "Everyone gets married! Who's going to take care of you?"

"Why can't I take care of myself?" Rose demanded.

"Ah, Rose, you can." Jacov spoke gently. "But what about babies?" Jacov was overjoyed at the thought of his own on the way. "Rose, don't you want little ones of your own? The Olshansky girls will make the best mothers I know."

Rose played with her hands on her lap. "I have lots of time to think about that, Jacov . . ." she said.

Meyer reached for his coat. "Not with Mume at work, you don't," he said under his breath.

The Songbird ⟿

Meyer stood with his arm around Anna and smiled as they watched Rose at the piano. It was a Neschvizer Sunday.

"Doesn't she have a lovely voice?" Meyer whispered.

"She seems to get better all the time. Her piano-playing, too. She should have lessons, Meyer," Anna answered.

"She doesn't need them. She learns all by herself."

"But she wants them, she always has," Anna said.

"She could probably have all she wants if she marries Levi Samuelson," Meyer said with a chuckle. "Look at him over there with Mume and Papa! Mume keeps jabbing him in the ribs, making him look at Rose!"

"Every Sunday she brings him," Anna sighed. "But

she won't let him dance with anyone but Rose. Not even little Becky Resnik! And remember last Sunday?"

Meyer grinned and nodded. "Who could forget?"

Levi had shyly asked Lister's daughter, who had been sitting at his table, if he could bring her something to eat. Mume had muttered—but loudly enough for everyone to hear—that Lister's daughter was a cow, who already had had enough to eat. Lister's wife had screamed at Mume, the daughter had burst into tears and the evening had ended abruptly, with the two families stalking off in different directions.

Now, everyone was back, but Mume and Lister's wife stayed on opposite sides of the big hall and glowered at each other whenever their eyes met.

"Rose is a good girl," Meyer said to his wife, "but I don't think Mume will be able to marry her off that easily. Anyway, she's got time. She's not quite fifteen."

"We fell in love when I was fourteen," Anna reminded him, "and you were fifteen-and-a-half."

"But Rose is not in love," Meyer said. "Look at her. She's having a wonderful time with just the music. She's not interested in dancing or talking with Levi or anyone else."

"Mmmm," Anna agreed and leaned her head against Meyer's shoulder.

Mikey Resnik, now a stocky little boy of eight, tugged at Rose's sleeve. "Play 'Casey Would Waltz,' Rose, play 'Casey Would Waltz.' Please? Please, Rose?"

"Next, Mikey, next," Rose said over her shoulder. "But don't pull my sleeve, it makes me miss the notes."

"Mikey!" Yette grabbed him by his shoulders. "Don't be such a *noodge*! Leave Rose alone. Go find Becky and Ruth. They're watching the little ones. You go help them!"

Rose glanced up and saw Mikey's face fall before he turned away. She stopped her song and swung into "And the Band Played On."

"Here it is, Mikey—just for you!" she called and the boy gave her a quick sad smile.

"Yette. Don't be so hard on the children," Rose said to her sister. "Soon you're going to be their mama. They work hard all week—this is a time for everyone to relax."

"You can say so," Yette retorted. "You don't have five small children underfoot every minute, fighting and screaming at each other."

"They're good children," Rose said. "And they've lost one mother. Don't give them such a scold to replace her."

"Don't preach at me, Rose Olshansky," Yette snapped. "*You're* going to have the life! A *young* man. A *rich* man. A chance to start your own family. Me, I get the castoffs, so don't tell me how to handle the children!"

Rose finished the song with a flourish and stood up.

"What are you talking about, Yette?" she demanded. "Who told you I was getting married?"

Yette was taken aback. "Everyone—everyone knows it," she said.

Rose's eyes flashed. " 'Everyone' knows it—except me! You know, Yette, it's very nice to have all your landsmen around you in a strange country, but the trouble with it is—everyone pokes his nose into your business and plans your life!"

"Everyone planned your life in the old country, too, Rose. Have you forgotten?"

"I was ten when we left the old country," Rose said, "and I did what my papa said. But maybe if we had stayed there I would have been just as angry when I got older at being told what to do."

"So—you aren't going to marry Levi Samuelson?" Yette asked.

"Yette, I'm not going to marry Levi Samuelson. We don't even know each other!"

"Well . . ." Yette gave Rose a rueful smile. "At least Papa and Mume won't have their way with one of us," she said.

"Yette—make yourself happy with Resnik and his children. They need you and they care for you. You've always been a mother to them . . ." Rose hugged her sister. She didn't know what else to say to her.

Yette pulled back. "Oh," she said, "Tudrus is crying. He's fallen. I must—" Her sentence trailed and she turned, moving through the crowd to go to the baby. Rose watched her retreating back. If Mume and Papa had only blessed a marriage between Levi and Yette, she thought, who knows? And was Levi what Yette really wanted after all? She shook her head.

Hinde touched Rose's shoulder and Rose jumped.

"Now what were you thinking so hard about?" Hinde asked. She was in her seventh month of pregnancy, but looked as if she were in her ninth.

Rose poked Hinde's belly lightly with her finger. "I

think you're going to have triplets, Hinde," she answered.

"Zena says maybe twins!"

"I wouldn't be at all surprised," Rose said. "Now, why don't you go and dance with your happy husband?"

"Dance!" Hinde looked horrified as she clutched at her huge belly. "Of all of us, Rose Olshansky, you were always the most *meshuganeh!*"

"Don't call my daughter crazy!" Mume barked as she sidled to the piano, dragging her brother by his arm. "Levi, listen how nice she plays!"

Rose stuck her tongue into her cheek to keep from laughing. *My daughter*, Mume had said. People claim and deny relatives as easily as they crush a sugar lump! Rose played a polka and the room rocked with the dancers.

Matchmakers 〰

"I have been a good father and given you time to think," Moshe said to Rose one night in late February. "Now you have thought. It is time to make a *shittoch* with Levi!"

"*A match? With Levi?*" Rose looked up from the tiny cape she was crocheting for Hinde's baby.

"This comes as no surprise to you, Rose. I have made my wishes clear. Do you hear me, daughter?"

Rose stared at him.

"Answer your father when he speaks to you!" Moshe boomed.

"You always say not to answer back," Rose said.

"Answer, I say!"

"I hear you, Papa," Rose answered.

"So?"

"So? No."

"*No!* You say 'no' to your papa?"

"Yes."

"*Yes,* then!"

"Yes, Papa, the answer is *no!* You're mixing me up."

"I am mixing *you* up! A child says no to her own father and that is mixing *you* up? I will not hear no, Rose. Levi Samuelson is—"

"—rich and young and a good match. I know, Papa. And he's also like a mouse, with no backbone. How could he have one with a sister like Mume?"

Moshe stepped forward and slapped Rose across her face. His fingers left white marks on her cheek. She barely blinked as she looked down at her needlework.

"I'm sorry, Papa," she whispered.

"Yes, you are sorry! Then it's settled."

"I am sorry I was so outspoken about Mume. I know you both mean well. But I will not be married off to Levi Samuelson or anyone else. I will work hard for you, Papa, all of my life, but I will not marry when and whom you tell me I will."

Moshe's ears reddened under his yarmulke. "You *will,* daughter," he said. "I say you *will.*" He slammed out of the Sklootses' flat.

As soon as the door closed with a bang, Lillian scurried out of her bedroom.

"I heard," she whispered, kneeling down next to Rose. "What will you do?"

Rose patted Lillian's hand. "Don't worry," she said.

"Don't worry! But, Rose—" Lillian began to cry. "This isn't the kind of marriage I always dream about for you and me. You have to do something—what will you do?"

Rose sighed and abandoned her work, letting it fall to the floor.

"I don't want to leave you all," she said thoughtfully. "But I could go away . . ."

At that, Lillian burst into real tears. "Oh, no, no, please," she sobbed, "Rose, please don't go away! Where would you go? And all alone? Oh, Rose, I'd never sleep again at night worrying about you. Please, Rose—"

"Oh, Lillian—" Rose stood and hugged her closest friend. "Lillian, don't cry. But do go back into your room and leave me alone for a while. I have to think."

"I'll help you!"

"No. Let me sit here by myself. The others will be back soon and I must make a plan. Go. Go now." She turned Lillian toward the bedroom door and the girl reluctantly left the kitchen.

Then Rose sat back down on her chair, folded her arms across her chest—and thought.

Hyman Rogoff ⌒

"Rose, things are getting exciting. The unions are about to make a big difference, not just here but in the whole country. You will see." Hyman took Rose's elbow as they crossed the street. He had picked her up directly after work.

Rose nodded absently. Her mind was not on the union.

"Mestrovich tells me he signed you up," Hyman said. "And your whole floor. Anna and Lillian have signed, too."

"Yes . . . What you told me made sense . . ." Rose said and rubbed at a blister on her finger.

"You joined because of what I said?" Hyman asked, smiling.

"Well." Rose straightened her shoulders. "Almost everyone has joined now. I mean . . . I suppose it's a good thing . . . to stand together."

"A good thing! It's the only way! The factory over in Brooklyn—Kahan's—the workers were out only two days and the foreman was fired!"

Rose kicked at a stone on the pavement.

"Did you hear me, Rose? Kahan's has a new fore-man now!"

"I know, I know," she sighed. "And this one tries to molest the women on the stairs."

"And who told you this!"

"Oh, Hyman, this is the new *shtetl*, only bigger. Everyone knows everything."

"Then *he* will be fired, too!" Hyman threw up his hands. "How is Warren reacting to all this?"

Rose looked at the sky. "Ach," she said. "It's going to snow."

"Rose. I asked you how is Warren reacting? To everyone's signing up? Has he said anything to you?"

Rose stopped walking. "Hyman Rogoff, did it ever

144

occur to you that more may be going on in my life than Mr. Warren's reaction to the union at Griffin?"

Hyman's lips parted as he frowned at her.

"No," she said with a laugh, "it hasn't occurred to you. Oh, Hyman, I don't want to talk about the union tonight!"

"Oh!" He quickly took her arm again. "All right . . . That's all right . . . I mean . . . What is it you want to talk about?"

"*Nothing!*"

"You don't want to talk about—anything?"

"Yes!"

"Oh."

They began to walk again. When they reached Rose's building, Hyman held onto her arm.

"You're behaving quite oddly tonight," he said. "Not like yourself. Usually you talk and talk!"

"Well, now I have to think and think."

Hyman stepped back. "Wouldn't you like to talk— I mean—I know there is something on your mind, Rose . . . Wouldn't you like to talk to me about it at all?"

Rose looked at his expression and her resolve nearly softened, but not quite.

"Thank you," she said stiffly. "But I do not want to talk. At all. Good night."

"Good night . . ."

She knew he hadn't turned and walked away as she climbed the stairs, and she felt sorry she had been so abrupt with him. For the first time, he had seemed sympathetic—actually interested in her and her thoughts.

She worked her way up to the Skloots flat. It was

nice, she thought, a nice side of him. But it wasn't important, at least right now.

The door was slightly ajar as Rose reached it and she could hear voices. For some reason she didn't understand, she stopped with her hand in midair—stopped herself from pushing the door open further. The voices were only mumbles, but then she heard:

"Enough. I've heard enough talking. My mind is made up. This will be settled and settled tonight." It was Moshe.

Now Zena: "Moshe, let the girl be, why can't you. She's fourteen, Moshe!"

"This one we can't let go. Levi is a prize," Moshe said.

Lillian: "But she doesn't want to, Mr. Olshanksy. She doesn't care for Mr. Samuelson. He hardly ever talks to her."

Moshe banged a fist on the table. "He's here every night! Every night she comes in too late! There is no control over the girl! It's time she got married and got all these American ideas out of her head!"

Rose, holding her breath, backed quickly away from the door and leaned against the wall.

"We make the *shittoch* tonight," Moshe boomed, "and we set the date *tonight*!"

Rose heard Zena's "Moshe, you're a fool," as she raced back down the stairs as quietly as she could.

Once outside, she looked from left to right, but she couldn't see Hyman. Never mind, she thought, he would probably be heading west, toward his flat. Or toward Mestrovich's—but still west. She began to run.

It didn't take her long to spot him. He had been

walking as slowly as she had been moving quickly.
There was that tall silhouette, wandering down the
street, out of the path of the crowd.

"Hyman!" she called and she saw him stop, turn.

"Rose?"

She raced toward him, reached him, and stood still.
Her mouth opened. She had no idea what she was
going to say.

"Rose?" he said again. "What is it? What's the matter? Is something wrong?"

"Hyman," she said, planting both feet together on
the sidewalk, "how do you feel about marriage?"

He stared at her.

"Well?"

"Uh," he said. "As an institution?"

"No. For you. And me."

"For you and me . . ."

"Stop repeating me! How do you feel about it?"

"Wait, uh—" He couldn't quite take in what she was
asking. "Just a minute," he managed. "Are you saying—"

"I am asking you a perfectly simple question. You
always have answers for everything. I will say it one
more time: How—do—you—feel—about—a—marriage
—between—*you*—" She pointed at him. "—and—*me?*"
She jabbed a forefinger at her own chest.

He started to smile. Then he began to laugh out
loud, while Rose stood watching him, her small face
angry and red.

"Well!" she said, inhaling deeply. "I guess you've
answered me!"

But he grabbed her as she turned. "No!" he cried.

147

"No, no, no! Rose—you must realize that this is a very surprising question!"

"Not necessarily," she retorted. "That's how it's done, isn't it? People say, 'Will you? You will. Fine, then it's settled!' So that's what I'm saying to you."

Hyman folded his arms. "You know, just a few minutes ago, you refused to talk to me about anything! That's what you said—'Thank you. But I do not want to talk.' From your very own mouth. And here you are, chasing me down the street, in front of all these people, asking me how I feel about marrying you! How do you expect me to react to that?"

In spite of herself, Rose began to giggle.

"You see? It's funny!"

"All right." She moved to lean against the wall of a store and he followed her. "I will start again, then," she said. "How do you think we would be together—married?"

He leaned toward her with that determined forward thrust of his body. "Good," he said finally. "I think we would be good. Together. Married. I have thought about it for a long time."

"You have?"

"Of course, I have! Why do you think I have been there every night for months, waiting for you, walking with you, hardly seeing my old friends! Why do you think that was?"

Rose thought. "Because you said I was different— and we had good talks. And arguments."

"I have good talks and arguments with Mestrovich!" he cried.

"Yes, but—"

"I *like* you, Rose Olshansky. I *admire* you. I—I—"

"What?"

"I—I *want* to marry you."

"You do?"

"Yes!"

"*I* think it's a terrible idea!" Rose blurted. "We would fight all the time. We have nothing in common, all our ideas are different, everything we want from life is different—"

"Stop!" he said, holding up his hand. "You asked me, remember?"

"I didn't ask you. I asked how you would feel about it. Why would you want to marry me if all we'd do is argue?"

"Because that's not all we'd do," he said.

Rose touched her hair with her hand.

"You have *direction*," he said softly. "And intelligence. And when you argue you have something to say. You have made me think. And you are . . . pretty."

"I'm not."

"You *are*! Do you want to get married or not?"

"If we had children we would fight over them all the time," she said, jutting out her jaw.

"Probably! Do you want to get married or not?"

"I still want to go to school!"

"I still think it's stupid! Do you want to get married or not!"

She stopped, panting as if she'd run a long way.

"Yes!" she said suddenly.

"Wonderful!" he cried.

They stared at each other.

Rose drew herself up. "All right, then," she said, finally. "I'll see you tomorrow," and she turned to go.

"Now, wait a minute," he said, falling into step with her. "What made you come running after me after you left me the way you did? Were you thinking about marriage while we were walking home? Was that why you didn't want to talk?"

Rose thought. She thought about telling him the truth or letting him think he had been on her mind all along. She bit her lip, took a breath and told him the truth.

"Tonight my father sets a date for me to marry my stepmother's brother. I heard them talking as I got to the door."

Hyman threw back his head. "Ah," he said. "I see."

"See what?"

"That I am the lesser of two evils. If you must get married, you would prefer that it be to me."

Rose said, "That's right."

"Then, you really don't feel . . . anything . . . for me."

"I didn't say that. I just agreed that if I have to get married then I would prefer that it be to you. I'd rather not be married, but then my father would run my life forever. So in order to be my own person, I must now begin my own family." She spoke clearly and without hesitation, but she could not look at him while she was talking.

Hyman repeated, "I see."

"If you don't approve of my reasons, I won't hold you to anything," Rose said quickly.

"No, no—I approve. I was just wondering if there might be . . . something else."

"Oh, no!" Rose cried, misunderstanding him. "I've told you the whole truth. I've left nothing out."

"Rose, what I meant was—was outside of the circumstances. What I meant was—your feelings. For me."

Rose cleared her throat. That was harder. She didn't know what her feelings were. In her mind, she tried to sort them out: Hyman was bright. He was passionately devoted to his beliefs. He was . . . reliable, she decided. After all, he never missed an evening to meet her.

And then she thought of Lillian. Sweet, fanciful Lillian, with her romantic dreams, her endless stream of chatter about . . . love. Love, moonlight, two people with eyes for only one another . . . Anna and Meyer, Hinde and Jacov, Lillian and some handsome someone whom she hadn't yet met . . . Lillian. Love.

Hyman waited. Rose thought.

Love. Lillian's idea of love was not hers, no matter how she tried to fuse their minds as she walked with Hyman Rogoff. But Lillian had not spent a year with Lowenstein, whose masculine scent Rose could still smell in nightmares. Lillian had known only Eli and Zena, two loving parents who had never been apart from their children. Moshe had gone from woman to woman until he'd settled here, with Mume, and had never shown the slightest interest in his children, except when it came to bending them to his will. Lillian could dream. Rose could not.

But Hyman—what *was* it about him?

Rose looked at him out of the corner of her eye and saw that he was watching her intently as they continued to walk. Hyman *respects* me, she thought. He listens to my thoughts and he cares enough to refute them! Even if he doesn't agree, he doesn't make me feel as if what I have said is unimportant!

"*That's* why I want to marry you!" she blurted.

"*Why?*" Hyman cried, and Rose laughed, realizing she had not been speaking aloud.

"Because you treat me like a person," she said simply.

"Ah," Hyman said, with an exaggerated nod of his head.

"Is that enough?" Rose asked.

"Enough for now," Hyman replied.

Saving Face ⌁

"*Who?*" Moshe bellowed, after Rose, with lowered eyes, told him her plans.

"Hyman Rogoff."

"The name, I don't care! A *buttonholemaker*! Hinde's Jacov has a shoe shop! Yette's Resnik has a grocery! And you find some *buttonholemaker*!"

"He's got a pushcart. He sells dry goods from that, too. He's a union organizer. He's a good—"

"Enough! I have already settled with Samuelson!"

"But I have not, Papa. We invite you to the wedding. You may come or not come. As you choose."

"I won't hear of it! You're too young! Fourteen is no age to marry!"

"Except to Levi Samuelson, Papa?"

"Yes! Except to Levi Samuelson! Because he can take care of you!"

"I can take care of myself, Papa. I can choose my own husband. We can take care of each other!"

Moshe stood in the Sklootses' kitchen and held out his arms. All the Sklootses were in their two bedrooms with their ears against the doors.

"Do you *hear?*" Moshe yelled at the top of his lungs. The Sklootses heard. The entire building heard. "Do you hear this girl? This unworthy girl with no respect for her *father?* Are there witnesses to this disrespect? I have no daughter!"

"Papa!" Rose grabbed at his jacket. "Papa, are you saying I'm *dead?* Are you *disowning* me, Papa?"

A gleam entered Moshe's eye. "And if I did?" he asked, cocking his head. "If I disowned you? What then?"

But Rose had caught the gleam. Now it was a game. She must win, but he could not think he had lost. A father could not lose face.

Quickly, she knelt at his feet.

"Papa, if you disowned me I would carry the guilt and shame for the rest of my life," she said, burying her face in her hands. "Not a night would I sleep for the rest of my life. And my every prayer would be for your forgiveness."

"*What?*" Moshe boomed, and Rose realized she must speak louder for the Sklootses and the neighbors to hear.

"*I would be shamed for the rest of my life!*" she cried to the walls. "*And I would still honor you, my father, forever!*"

"Aha!" Moshe said, and patted her once, hard, on the top of her head. "That is how a daughter should feel!"

Rose gathered her skirts and stood up. "Then I can have your blessing, Papa?" This last she whispered.

"I will meet him. Tomorrow."

"Yes, Papa. Of course."

"No. Not tomorrow. Tonight!"

"Yes, Papa."

"*Then* I will decide."

"Yes, Papa." Rose rushed from the room, Hyman was waiting downstairs. But before hurrying down to him, she leaned heavily against the stair rail in the hall, swaying slightly. Her eyes rolled up and she let out her breath through puffed cheeks.

"I did it," she said. Twice. In English and in Yiddish. "I did it! Thank you, God, amen."

Rose in June ⟞

And so, early in the summer of 1898, Hyman Rogoff crushed to tiny shards the symbolic glass beneath his feet, concluding the ceremony that united him and Rose Olshansky in marriage before all her family and their friends.

SEVEN

1899

A Gleam in Her Eye ⟿

Rose's eyes shone as she listened to Mr. Pratt describing a society party he and his sister were to attend in the spring. Rose often paused to chat with her teacher when class was over, not only because she admired him, but to better copy his American accent and improve her vocabulary. Besides, Hyman usually worked very late—sometimes until ten o'clock. Rose tried to get him to relax at least one evening a week at the men's poker game, but Hyman told her she was better at cards—he would work.

". . .and in addition, there is to be a twenty-piece orchestra to play through dinner and dancing," Mr. Pratt was saying.

Dinner, Rose noted. Not supper. "Twenty musicians? How wonderful!" Rose closed her eyes. "I am picturing," she said, "how beautiful the ladies will look as they slide around the floor . . ."

"As they *glide*," Mr. Pratt said.

" '*Glide,*' " Rose repeated. "*Slide* sounds slippery. *Glide* is . . . is *floating.*"

"Good!" Mr. Pratt said with a smile.

"*Glide, slide* . . . One letter, but a big difference. I will get it."

"You will."

"Tell me what your sister plans to wear to this party!" Rose said. "Tell me all about her dress!"

"Gown," Mr. Pratt said.

"Gown?"

"A gown *is* a dress, Rose, but it is for formal wear. A dress is something a woman can wear every day."

Rose nodded. "Tell me about her *gown,* then," she said, and whispered to herself, "gown."

"Well! It's funny you should mention that, because Irene was saying this morning that she'd like to have one made, but she wasn't quite sure what she wanted."

"I have often imagined a beautiful society dress—*gown*—" Rose said. "While I'm playing the piano on Sundays at Neschvizer, sometimes I make up—*design*—gowns . . . for dressing up . . . And I make believe all my family dancing around me is wearing them . . ."

"Describe one for me."

"Oh. Well. It would be cut like—so—" She indicated bare shoulders and low-cut bodice. "And very tight to the waist—here— and coming to a little point. With embroidered roses, dotted with tiny seed pearls, from here to here . . . This gown I see in a pale peach color— yards and yards of silk, lace here—"

"Rose, can you draw it?" Mr. Pratt asked.

She tried, but in the end, Irene Pratt herself came down to the night school one evening and Rose "acted the dress out" for her, pantomiming the sleeves, the bodice, the way it would hang from the waist. Irene Pratt was impressed.

"Do make it for me, Rose," she begged. "Whatever the materials cost—you must make it exactly the way you've described it!"

Moshe Olshansky's gleam appeared in his daughter's eye. Whatever the materials cost! Imagine being able to say that!

Very well, Miss Pratt, Rose said to herself. You will have the most beautiful gown at your big society party with your twenty-piece orchestra! And if money doesn't matter, I will be able to work magic for you. And start a bit of a nest egg besides!

Love and Marriage ~~~

Patterns and materials were spread across the bed in Rose's and Hyman's cramped one-room flat and Rose busied herself with them as she talked with Lillian, perched on a wooden stool in the corner.

"The trouble with marriage," Rose was saying, "is that we never get to see each other! We're at our jobs during the day, I've got this gown to make for Miss Pratt, there's school and studying—Hyman's pushing his cart until all hours—hand me those pins, please, Lillian?"

Lillian reached for a pincushion and handed it to Rose.

"And not only that," Rose continued, ". . . there's going to be a baby. In August, I think."

"*What?*" Lillian leaped from her stool, causing a breeze to ruffle Rose's paper patterns.

"Careful!" Rose cried, laughing.

"But why didn't you say something before? That's—" Lillian ticked off time on her fingers— "only six months away! Rose, why didn't you tell me? Why did—"

"Lillian, I wasn't sure. I really wasn't. I—I've never done this before, you know . . ." She smiled as Lillian threw her arms around her neck.

"Oh, but, Rose, shouldn't you be resting? All this work—in your condition—does Hyman know? Oh, but of course he knows—Rose, lie down! Rest! How can you do all this? Anna was exhausted all the time!"

Anna and Meyer's new son, Dovid, was just a month old.

"I'm all right," Rose assured Lillian. "I seem to have all the energy I need for work. I really think it's because of the baby I have the strength. Hand me the scissors."

"Ah, you make me feel guilty," Lillian sighed. "I left the work I was doing for Papa to come and visit with you. I hate to think of you all alone when Hyman is out so late . . ."

"I am fine, Lillian. But I'm always glad to see you. Tell me about life at the Sklootses'. I do miss you and Zena and Eli."

"Things are much the same," Lillian said lightly. "And there is the poker game. Lately it's been at our house all the time. Hinde is always afraid Moshe's bellowing over a poor hand will wake Baby Esther."

Rose laughed. "Baby Esther will learn to sleep through Papa's bellowing just as we did when we were babies."

"Levi Samuelson always comes with Moshe. I think he's very nice . . ."

"Do you? Tell me, has Levi finally found words?"

"Oh, Rose! Of course he has words. Not like his sister's, to be sure!"

"Oh, good. Mume's words we'd rather not hear!"

"Levi's very quiet, it's true. But the other night, when I brought him cake, he touched my fingers and he didn't move his hand away when he said, 'Thank you so much, Lillian' . . ."

"Well! That's quite a long sentence for our Levi! You should hear Hyman and me—sometimes we have to stamp our feet to let the other know we want to get a word in!" She stopped when she saw Lillian's face fall. My sweet friend, she thought, I hope you never wake up from your world of dreams.

"I hear footsteps on the stairs, Rose," Lillian said. "Hyman must be home!"

Rose rolled her eyes as the doorlatch clicked. "Oh, and there's no room to move in here," she moaned.

Hyman shuffled in and wearily raised his arms.

"Ach, Rose—look at the bed! Papers, materials, needles, thread, pins—I wanted to lie right down and go to sleep! Such a day—I'm so tired I don't remember putting away the cart."

Rose's lips twitched in a smile. "Say hello to Lillian, Hyman," she said.

"Oh, I'm sorry. Hello, Lillian."

"Hello, Hyman . . . And congratulations!"

"Eh?"

"The baby, Hyman! Your coming baby!"

"The baby. Yes. The baby. Thank you."

Rose began to gather up her things from the bed. "You see, Lillian?" she said, still smiling. "*This* is marriage. A little room, a lot of work, a baby to think about—you must keep your feet on the ground. Aren't your feet on the ground, Hyman?"

"They are now, but I want to put them on the bed."

Lillian laughed. "What about supper, Hyman? Let me get it for you before I leave. Rose has soup on the stove over there—I tasted it. It's wonderful!"

But Hyman just closed his eyes and shook his head.

The First Birthday ➤

Outside, the April air was mild and sweet, but inside Hinde and Jacov's kitchen it felt stuffy. Especially with all the people gathered there. Meyer loosened his tie as he studied Hyman Rogoff sitting stiffly next to the only window. What a husband Rosele chose, Meyer thought. She's a little songbird and he—he is like a watchdog, never letting his guard down for a moment. So serious always!

"Hyman!" Rose called to him. "You must taste Zena's mandelbreit this minute while it's at its flakiest!"

"Rose, you have stuffed me enough," Hyman protested, but he took the thin cake from her fingers and dutifully ate while murmuring appreciation.

Rose patted her growing belly and smiled at her husband. "If I am looking stuffed, why shouldn't you?" she laughed.

It was a birthday party. Esther Abramson—named for Jacov's mother—was one year old, and Hinde and Jacov had invited the family to celebrate the occasion.

"Birthday!" Moshe snorted loudly. "Who has a celebration for a birthday!"

"We do, Papa," Hinde said firmly, patting her father's shoulder. "Now and from now on. None of us ever knew our own, but we know Esther's. April 14th!"

"And Dovid Olshansky's!" Celia cried. "Dovid will be four months old next week!" Celia felt terribly important—a real aunt to two babies!

"Please let me hold Dovid," Celia begged Anna. "I want him to watch Esther and see what his own first birthday party will be like!" She reached for the baby boy and took him with Anna's usual warning to be careful and support his bottom!

Meyer, with an absent smile at Celia, thought about his family gathered around him. All still here—and still alive. Still poor, too, but all in all, he couldn't complain. He and Anna were still cramped in Lister's extra room, but after his years in a horsecart, how could he grumble! And little Dovid! It was a shock to Moshe and to Eli, too, that they had named their son for no deceased relative! They had broken all tradition. They had simply liked the name and given it to their son. Zena had cried a little—she'd had her heart set on "Israel," named for her own mother, Ida. But Anna had wailed, "No, no, all the children will call him 'Izzy' or 'Ikey'!" So Zena had relented and, of course, adored her first grandchild, no matter his name.

Meyer looked up as Hinde laughed aloud at something Eli said. Jacov and Baby Esther had certainly changed Hinde from a tight-mouthed, high-strung girl to a warm and loving woman.

Now Yette, Meyer thought, as he glanced at his second-oldest sister. She was busy scolding Ruth Resnik while keeping a watchful eye on young Mikey at the food table. Yette, Meyer felt, had also changed but not for the better. There were lines of fatigue and bitterness etched around her mouth and her eyes always seemed red and watery. Anna had whispered to Meyer that she was sure Yette was pregnant, although nothing showed. In any case, if it were true, Yette didn't seem happy about it. Not at all.

"Meyer, look at Dovidle!" Celia called to him. "Look at your little son!" She held the baby up and put her cheek next to his. "Look, Meyer, this is your face! Your very own—whenever you get tired and cranky!"

Meyer laughed. "I never get tired and cranky, Celia," he called to her. "Just ask Anna!"

Celiale, Meyer thought. A big girl now, and so proud of her niece and nephew! In June, she and Fanny would be leaving school to take their places among the salary-earning women of the family. No bar mitzvah, like for the boys, but a graduation into adulthood, nonetheless.

And then there was Rose. Rosele, Meyer's favorite.

He looked at her now. Rose Olshansky Rogoff, almost sixteen years old and very much a woman—going to be a mama herself now. Meyer watched Rose push a piece of sugar bun into little Esther's mouth. He waved his fingers at her.

"You'll make her chubby like her Tante Rose if you're not careful," Meyer teased. Rose made a face at him and he laughed. Look at her, Meyer thought. Round little *punim* and a body to match! Rose was never thin, but now . . .! Still, always bright, moving as if she heard music playing everywhere she went.

"I wish you had a piano, Hinde!" Rose called at that moment, confirming her brother's thoughts. "Esther should be learning to dance at her first birthday!" Meyer beamed to himself.

"Why are you smiling to yourself like that, Meyer Olshansky?" It was Lillian Skloots at his elbow. "You're not allowed to have your own little private jokes at a family celebration. You must share everything."

"Everything, Lillian? Surely you have some little secrets of your own, don't you?"

"Oh, Meyer!" Lillian blushed. It wasn't really a secret that Levi Samuelson continued to visit the Skloots flat, though no longer at Moshe's behest.

A Promise of More 〜

"Hyman! You'll never guess!"

"What, Rose? Tell me!"

"Miss Irene Pratt wore the gown I designed to her big fancy party!"

"Ah, Rose! I know that! Didn't you sit up round the clock, night after night, making that dress?"

"*Gown*, Hyman, *gown*! And yes, of course I did, but—"

"And didn't Miss Irene Pratt pay you a nice sum for your work?"

"Yes, Hyman, yes, but—"

"Then what, Rose? What, then?"

"Mr. Pratt told me his sister was the 'belle of the ball'!"

"Yes?"

"Yes! She outshone everyone in her peach silk!"

"Rose! I'm proud of you!"

"But, Hyman, there's more! Listen! All the ladies at the party wanted to know *where* Miss Irene Pratt had her gown made!"

"Ahhhhh!"

"And many of them now want me to sew gowns for *them*!"

"Ahhhhhhhh!"

"And, Hyman . . . even though I've left the factory, I can be making money! And more than before! And do you know what that means? We'll be able to move to a bigger flat before the baby is born! A flat with a separate bedroom, Hyman!"

"Ahhhhhhhhhh!"

A Birth ⌒

In the Rogoff's new two-room flat on Rivington Street, somewhere between one and two-thirty in the morning on August 20, 1899, Baby Boy Rogoff pushed screaming into the world.

"A boy!" Zena beamed at an exhausted Rose, bathed in sweat on the bed. "A boy, Rose! And hollering at his own arrival! What will you call him?"

"Zena . . ."

"What? Yes—" Zena bent over and put her ear to Rose's mouth.

"It's a healthy baby?"

"Healthy, Rose. He's fine."

Rose smiled. "Hyman?"

"In the next room, playing cards with Eli."

"Playing cards? At a time like this?"

Zena laughed. "Don't worry. Eli won't make him pay what he's lost. So far it's the pushcart and everything on it!"

"His name . . ." Rose said weakly.

"Yes? The name?"

Bonny ⌒

The name on the birth certificate that Zena filled out and gave to the authorities was "Bonny." Rose had meant "Barney," a name she had heard at night school and liked. It was actually a sort of nickname, or shortening of the name "Bernard," but Rose didn't know that. Rose had liked "Barney," and with her accent, Zena and the birth-records people had heard "Bonny." And Bonny, he was.

Yette couldn't come to the *pidyen-a-ben*, the ceremony of the circumcision. Anna had been right. Yette had been pregnant but she'd lost the baby just before Bonny's birth. Rose was torn between her own happiness and Yette's loss. Recovering on Rivington Street, she couldn't even visit her sister.

"It's good you can't go, Rose," Hinde told her. "Yette cries all the time. The house is full of sorrow and anger, Rose. Those children—"

"What about the children? Mikey?" Rose had always had a soft spot for Mikey Resnik.

"They were good children once, but now—Becky. She stays out late. Yette doesn't know where she goes. Mikey—he's with those Homowitz boys. They have a gang—they steal—"

"Mikey? Little Mikey?"

"Little Mikey. Not even ten yet. Yette has no control, she doesn't even try to control. If you go there your milk will sour, Rose. The rest of us go. Myself, Anna—Celia and Fanny go to help. But Yette doesn't care."

"Yette is stuck inside herself, Hinde. She has chosen to see her life as bad. Still, this city is so hard on young children. If their mama is busy . . . what is there for them to do? It's easy to find trouble in these streets. Hinde, I wish I could help . . ."

"You can't. Yette is too bitter. Besides, you have a child of your own to take care of now."

A Call on Rivington Street ⌒

There were other visitors to Rivington Street. Lillian came, clutching Levi's hand.

"Such a beautiful baby, Rose! The very best of you and Hyman! Isn't he just *beautiful*, Levi?"

"He's fat, like me," Rose said. "He has four chins."

"No, not four!" Lillian laughed. "But babies are supposed to be fat. Mama always says so, doesn't she, Levi? Fat babies are healthy babies, Mama says. Oh, Rose, I just can't believe it—your very own baby! I'm an aunt again, aren't I, Levi? Oh, not by blood, maybe, but I shall always think of myself as Bonny's real aunt—"

"Of course you're his real aunt!" Rose said, struggling to sit higher in the bed. "He couldn't have a closer aunt than you, Lillian, and I couldn't have a closer sister! Now, let Levi hold that baby for a minute," Rose told her. "I think he's too heavy for you, Lillian!"

"He certainly isn't—but here, Levi! See what it feels like!" Lillian carefully handed Bonny to Levi, whose eyes widened in fear. "Come on, now . . . He won't break . . ."

Levi's whole body was stiff, but he cradled Bonny tenderly and grinned so hard at Rose and Lillian that they both had to laugh!

And Moshe and Mume came, too, bringing bread and cakes.

"Oy, is he fat!" was Mume's comment as she slapped the side of her face.

Rose bridled. "Babies are supposed to be fat," she said. "Zena says so."

"It means he's healthy!" Moshe barked and glared at his wife. "And where's that father of his, that man you married! He leaves you alone at night, Rose, to go talking unions with his friends?"

"No, Papa," Rose answer calmly. "Hyman works every night. He collects things for his cart, he sells . . . He works very hard every day and at night, too, Papa."

"I knew! He's a good man. I made you a good match, Rose!"

Now it was Mume's turn to frown and Rose hid a smile behind her fingers.

A Good Bargain ⌒

A Sunday in November. Rose was busily at work on a silk gown for another of Miss Pratt's friends. Hyman was folding embroidered tablecloths to pile on his pushcart. He yawned loudly.

"Hyman, don't sell today," Rose begged, licking the end of her thread. "Rest. And we'll go to Neschvizer later together with the baby."

"I'd rather sell than go to Neschvizer today," Hyman replied. "It's nice weather for this time of year, not cold at all. People will be out and Sunday is always good for business, Rose."

"But that's why I want to go! It will be Bonny's first visit and I want everyone to see him. I want to watch him with you, I want Papa to watch him with you, I want you to hold him near the piano when I play so he can hear the instrument for the first time. Oh, Hyman, it's my only real break in the week, except for night school."

Hyman made a face as he always did when Rose

mentioned school. The table was piled high with books in a language he didn't understand.

"Night school!" he snorted. "Yesterday a man spoke on the street. Karl Marx's theory of surplus value, the theory of class struggle, the inevitability of socialism—the crowd cheered, Rose! A new world is coming and our son will be a part of it. Night school! What did you get from night school? Some nice money for the clothes you make for the teacher! More sewing, that's what you got from night school! You prove my point!"

"That's an extra, Hyman! Look at these books. I can read Dickens. And Shakespeare, the greatest playwright who ever lived! I can understand them. I can escape from this world into another, and you'd feel better if you could do that, too. But all you think about is work and your union. Take Bonny to Neschvizer with me, Hyman. Let him hear the music . . . see the dancing . . . spread his wings—" She waved her arm and knocked a book and a cup from the table. "Ach, a bigger flat and we're still cramped!"

"Of course. A new addition to the family does that to an apartment. Even though his wings are a little too small to spread at the moment . . ."

"Hyman, you know what I mean. Music will open his mind no matter how small he is. Music is wonderful for babies, Hyman! Bonny might turn out to be a great composer in your new world!"

"*Composer*! What good is a composer of music?"

"His music would make others happy. There is good in that."

"A composer does not change the ills of society!"

"Nothing can change the ills of society. A composer can make them bearable."

"But, Rose, of course you can change society! Your thinking is what sets us back! Man creates his evils and man can uncreate them!"

"I'm uncreating them my way! I'm trying to live my life with a little beauty and culture. You discount the value of that!"

Hyman threw up his hands. "Now I *am* too tired to sell!" he cried. "The same argument, Rose!"

"The same argument. Poor little Bonny will be torn to shreds between us."

"No, he won't." Hyman softened his voice. "No, he won't, Rose. He will have the best of us both."

"The best of us both," Rose said. "That's what Lillian said . . . 'the very best of you and Hyman' . . ."

"Lillian is right—the boy is blessed," Hyman said with a smile. "Now let's not argue any more. It's Sunday, after all. And I do want to take advantage of this weather with the cart . . ." He yawned again.

"Poor Hyman," Rose said. "I know you're tired . . ."

"And I know you want to go to Neschvizer," Hyman said.

"All right," Rose said, "let's do this: You take the cart for a while and I will finish my work. After lunch, you take Bonny for a stroll in the park and then both of you come back here and have a good nap while I go to Neschvizer. Is that a good bargain?"

"It sounds like a fine bargain. But I thought you wanted to take Bonny—"

"Not without you. I want us to be together for his

first meeting with his landsmen. Besides, as you said, the weather is nice. He needs the fresh air."

"The fresh air smells a lot like stale cooking," Hyman said, "but I agree. And Bonny and I will be sleeping soundly when you return from the party."

Off in a Carriage ⬎

Rose had Bonny packed into the grand carriage the Pratts had given them for a baby present, and she was standing next to it in the hall when Hyman returned from pushing his cart.

"We're both ready," she said. "You don't have to do a thing. Give Bonny his fresh air and then come straight back here and nap with him. I'm off to meet Lillian on the corner. All right?"

Hyman looked at her stocky little form before him. "And if I said 'not all right'?" he joked. "Maybe Bonny and I will take our nap right now, eh?"

"Oh, Hyman . . . please take him now while it is still nice. There are clouds and it may rain later. And he must have his daily fresh air."

"That is an old wives' tale, Rose."

"No, no, it's true. Please take him now, Hyman. Please?"

He could never resist her when she said "please." She so rarely did.

"Yes, yes," he sighed, "we are going. Bonny and I are going for daily fresh air. Now, pick him up and carry him so I can get the carriage down the stairs easier. Please?"

A Change of Weather ➤

When Rose returned from the Neschvizer, it was raining. The gathering had broken up earlier than usual because of the storm—a wind had arisen from the north, causing the rain to freeze and turn to sleet. Rose was glad Hyman had taken the baby out during the warm part of the day.

The flat was dark when Rose let herself in. She lit the gas lamp and wondered why Hyman had not left it on for her. She tiptoed into their bedroom and suddenly her insides were as cold as the storm outside. Hyman was not in bed, Bonny was not in his cradle.

Rose fought her panic. Hyman must have gone to a relative's, she thought. But no—they had all been at Neschvizer! Mestrovich's? No. No, Hyman was tired. He wanted to go to bed. Besides, he never would keep the baby out in this weather—never.

She began to run around the tiny flat, her hands fluttering. She had no idea where to begin to look for them—

She flung open the door and yelled into the dim hall: "Hyman! Hyman Rogoff!" No one answered. Rose began to bang on the neighbors' doors, running from one flat to the other without bothering to wait until they answered.

"Please—have you seen Hyman? Have you seen the baby carriage?" she cried in the darkened hall.

Doors opened. Faces looked at her blankly.

"Hyman's not home?" Mrs. Lublin asked.

"The carriage is not in the hall—" Rose was sobbing now. "Doesn't anyone know—"

"Rose, Rose come inside. Have some tea," Mrs. Aronson begged. "They are safe, they just stayed too long somewhere. They will come home when it stops raining. Don't get so upset, Rose . . ."

It made sense to Rose, but it calmed her only a little. Fear still nagged and her stomach was churning.

Suddenly the downstairs door banged shut. Rose leaned over the railing and yelled as loud as she could, not caring if the entire building heard her.

"Hyman! Hyman! Is that you!"

No one answered her, but the heavy sound of booted feet on the stairs came closer and closer.

Rose and all the neighbors still in their doorways gasped together, as Hyman, drenched to his toes and clutching Bonny in soaked blankets, finally reached the landing.

For once, Rose couldn't speak. Hyman said nothing, either, but he pushed his way past her into their flat. He seemed not to have seen her.

Rose raced after him, grabbing the baby from his arms as he stood there, dripping ice and water on the floor.

The only sounds were Rose's little sobs as she tended to the baby, undressing him, heating water to make a bath for him, wrapping him in dry blankets, holding him to give him her own body warmth.

Only when Bonny began to cry and wave his tiny fists did Rose feel any relief. She looked over at Hyman, who had sunk into a kitchen chair.

"Undress," she said to him. "Get out of those clothes,

don't just sit there." Mrs. Aronson had brought some schnapps and Rose poured a little into a glass.

Hyman's teeth were chattering and Rose saw his hands shaking as he tried to undo a button. With Bonny wrapped and warm, she put him into his cradle and hurried to her husband.

"Drink this," she said, holding the glass of liquor to his lips. "Look at you—fingers practically frozen," she scolded as she got him out of his clothes. "Into bed. Quick!" She began to pull out all the feather beds and quilts they had received as wedding presents.

Under the covers, his teeth still chattering, Hyman spoke for the first time.

"N-Never asked me," he mumbled.

"What?"

"You n-never asked m-me what h-happened," he managed.

"So?" she said. "What happened?"

Hyman smiled in spite of himself. It was so like Rose—what happened would come later. First, do what had to be done.

"F-fell asleep. In the p-park. Was not c-cold—warm, even. Sat on a b-bench—fell asleep—B-Bonny in the carriage—fell asleep—"

"You slept in the rain?" Rose asked, her eyes widening.

"N-never fel-felt the rain . . . Bonny cried—woke me—r-ran all the w-way home—holding him—left the carriage—t-take too long to p-push—"

"Oh, Hyman—"

It wasn't until his shivering stopped and he slept that Rose began to cry.

Recovery ⟶

Hyman recovered from pneumonia, but after three weeks, when they were sure the crisis had passed, a strange thing happened. All of his hair fell out. It came out on his pillow, in his hairbrush, even when he touched his head. Tufts of it were left in his hand. He and Rose stared at the handfuls of hair and then at each other in shock.

"It will grow back," Rose assured him. But it didn't. Hyman Rogoff was completely bald at twenty-one.

Throughout Hyman's illness, Rose had watched Bonny like a hawk, but the baby seemed to suffer only a bad cold and had stopped sneezing and coughing after only a week. Everyone had helped. Celia and Fanny had taken Hyman's pushcart out. Hinde had made pot after pot of chicken soup. Even Mume, scolding and complaining, had stayed with Hyman and Bonny so Rose could run her errands. Yette sent groceries from Resnik's over with Becky and Ruth, who helped by bringing steaming pots of water into the bedroom to help the invalids breathe better.

At last it ended. Bonny seemed fine. Hyman, still bearded, though his head was bare, had been left weakened by his month-long illness. He looked years older than he was.

Rose, however, seemed to gain strength with every passing day. If Hyman's chin lost its jut of resolution, Rose's grew firmer. She worked harder, but her mind was elsewhere. Hyman would hear her muttering to herself, even while she sewed or tended to him or the baby.

"What was that?" he would ask. "What did you say?"

"Mr. Pratt doesn't live like this. He has a warm house. With many rooms. A yard, Hyman. He could put his baby out in the yard for air and watch him from a window."

"I thought Mr. Pratt wasn't married."

"He's not. I was only saying."

"*What* were you saying?"

"There's better," Rose answered. "There's better than this."

Strike ⟋⟍

In the second week of December, the Griffin Cap Factory was struck by pieceworkers. Lillian Skloots wasn't marching with the other women from her floor, but she was standing on the sidewalk watching them when the fights broke out. The foreman, Mr. Warren, had hired scabs, and as they made their way into the building to go to work, the angry strikers began to hit them with their signs.

Fascinated, Lillian moved nearer the wall, standing on tiptoes and peering over the heads of the crowd to see better. The police arrived and began using their clubs to separate the fighters. One of the policemen, raising his club on a backswing, smashed Lillian's head. He hadn't seen her.

Two of the women strikers carried Lillian home.

She lived for three days but never regained conscious-ness. She never knew that Rose had not left her bed-side, had slept intermittently, holding Lillian's hand the entire time, had not eaten, had left her husband and baby in the care of neighbors, had stood and walked for the first time only when she was sure that Lillian was no longer breathing.

Levi Samuelson was there with her. This time Rose did not mind his silence, she welcomed it. Levi was as stricken as Rose and his face and body communicated his helplessness and misery.

When Rose let go of Lillian's hand and stood up, Levi gasped loudly.

"*Lillian?*" he cried.

Rose moved to hold him.

"She was—she was—" Levi stammered as Rose put her arms around him. "She was my words," Levi whis-pered. "My voice. I was about to—I was just about to ask her to marry me, Rose. Do you think she knew that? Do you think she knew it, Rose?"

The others were there: Zena, Eli, Anna, Meyer . . . They were all there. They clutched at each other, shared their grief, rent their clothing, mourned. Not Rose. Rose picked up her shawl, left the Sklootses' flat and went home to Hyman and Bonny.

A Good Place ⌁

Hyman looked at her face and knew. He could only shake his head from side to side, slowly, sorrowfully.

177

"Your union," Rose said.

'Ahhh, Rose. It wasn't the union. You know better. Don't do that, Rose, you'll be blaming *me*."

"I don't blame you," she said. Her usually musical voice was dull. Flat. "I don't blame the union, at least not directly. But Lillian shouldn't have died, Hyman. Lillian should have lived with romance and music and . . . and flowers blooming in her path. She should have had mountains to look at, with clouds hanging over their tops—a place to make her dreams grow! No dreams grow here, Hyman! This is cement and poverty and fights and crowded, cramped rooms with no air or light!"

Rose went to her husband, put her arms around him and rested her head against his shoulder.

"This isn't enough, Hyman," she said. "There has to be more. More space for Bonny to grow. In all ways, Hyman. This is a box we have put ourselves in."

He stroked her bright soft hair. "You can't run away from life, Rose," he said.

"Oh, I know that! But you can run away from one life to another one. There are better lives! My books have told me—my teacher has shown me—and my heart has shouted at me! Hyman, we can live under these conditions, we have lived under worse conditions—but we will not grow." She broke away from him and went to her kitchen drawer.

"What are you doing?" Hyman asked.

From the back of the drawer, she pulled out a tin that had once contained tea and opened it. She pulled out some money, held it in her fist and waved it at him.

178

"Three dollars," she said.

"So?"

"Bonny and I will go to the railroad station."

"The railroad station? You mean uptown?"

"Hyman, of course uptown. That's where the station is. I can find it, don't worry. I'm going much further away than the railroad station!"

"To *where*, Rose? Where? Away from me? You're taking Bonny away from me?"

"No, Hyman. Away from this. Away from what Yette's become, away from what Mikey Resnik's become, away from street gangs and union fights and needless deaths—"

"But, Rose, what about Hinde? Hinde and Jacov, Meyer and Anna—they have children, they are happy, they are making do . . ."

"Yes, Hyman, that's just it! They are making do! They are going along, along the path that my father and all the other fathers made for them . . . They all still live in a ghetto.

"In Neschviz there was space . . . We were poor, but there were trees. When I came here, there was no space, but I thought: At least there will be no pogroms. I will not be struck down and killed. Now I am not sure. Lillian was killed . . . There are many ways of being killed, Hyman."

Hyman looked at her, clutching the money in her tight fist.

Rose drew herself up. "I looked at Lillian's face when she died. Except for that awful purple color under her bandage, she looked as if she were sleeping. I once prayed that Lillian would never have to wake up from her dreams and now she won't. But I can do more. I can make dreams real.

"I'm not leaving you, Hyman, I'm only going away. I don't know how long it will take me to get work when I get off that train, but I will get it. My hands can make beautiful things and I will get work. And until I have a business going, you must stay here. Keep your factory job and keep your pushcart. Give up this flat and stay with Eli or Mestrovich. Save all the money you can. And by then I will be ready, with money I've saved and a good place to live. And you will come join us, our baby and me."

He looked at her for a long time without speaking. He knew there was nothing he could say. This had been inside her always. It was what had attracted him in the first place. He knew he couldn't hold her, wouldn't want to.

"When will you go?" he asked.

"Tomorrow morning."

"Lillian's funeral. The week of *shive*—"

"No. I don't need to sit on a crate for a week to mourn for Lillian. I will mourn for Lillian all of my life. I'm going tomorrow."

At Grand Central Station

Rose sat down on a bench and let Bonny slip to her lap. She put her small suitcase—the same one she'd kept from the boat voyage so long ago—next to her on the floor, along with a small package of food she'd packed.

"An-so-nee-a," Rose crooned to the baby. "It's musical, isn't it, Bonny?"

The baby gurgled in his sleep. Rose unbuttoned his little coat to make him more comfortable and it was then she saw, pinned to his sweater—five dollar-bills.

Oh, Hyman, she breathed.

Five dollars. It took him two days to make that with the pushcart. Tears filled her eyes.

She unpinned the money and slipped it into her coat pocket. She had brought enough food for herself and Bonny to last at least this day. As soon as she got off the train she was planning to find a place to live where she could earn her keep and not pay rent. But still—it was good to have the security of those five dollar-bills ... A good man, Rose thought. A very good man.

Ansonia. Bonny will take his first steps on grass. He will go all through school—all through *high school*! I will have a piano and Bonny will take lessons ...

Rose smiled. I sound like you, Lillian—daydreaming like this. Wouldn't you laugh to hear me! Except I can do it. It will be real, Lillian. Watch me, Lillian ... I'll do it for both of us ...

Rose closed her eyes. Little Celia, she thought. She will be sad that I'm gone, but it won't be long before we see each other again. And she has Fanny, close as a sister, close as Lillian and I ... Goodbye, Celia. Goodbye, Meyer—take good care of Anna and Dovid ... and Hyman, too ... Goodbye, Hinde, Jacov, Yette, Papa, Mume, Zena, Eli ... We will meet again in the open air, I promise. I promise ...

Rose hadn't thought she'd slept, but it seemed like no time at all before she heard: "Shel-ton! Der-by! An-son-ia! Now boarding on track sixteen—"

Rose stuck the ticket in her mouth, picked up her baby and her baggage, took a deep breath and marched forward.

The seat was hard, the material covering it worn through, and the windows were greasy, but Rose noticed none of it. She pressed her nose to the glass, watching the city fall further and further behind.

When? she asked herself. How long? How many more miles of tracks before I can see ... before we can see ...

"Ahh!" Rose said aloud. A fat man across the aisle looked up from his newspaper to peer at her, but she paid him no attention. She was too busy staring through the train window.

Bonny woke up from his nap and blinked his eyes at her.

"Just in time, Bonny!" Rose said as she held him up. "You woke up just in time! Look!" She turned the baby so that his face was next to hers, so that he, too, faced the window. "Trees, Bonny! Real trees! Country, Bonny! Space and sky!"

Bonny wrinkled up his face and yawned. Rose laughed and kissed his pudgy cheek.

"Keep looking, Bonny," she said. "Keep looking out there. Ahead of you."